During and afte[r] ... offi[c]er in the [...] inte[l]ligence dutie[s ...] adve[r]tising agency, a farmer, managing director of a pirate radio station, and a PR consultant. He now lives in Lamb[e]rhurst, Kent, with his family.

M000076450

By the same author

TED ALLBEURY

Consequence of Fear

GRANADA
London Toronto Sydney New York

Published by Granada Publishing Limited in 1981
Reprinted 1982 (twice)

ISBN 0 583 12937 4

First published in Great Britain by
Granada Publishing Limited 1979
Copyright © Ted Allbeury 1979

Granada Publishing Limited
Frogmore, St Albans, Herts AL2 2NF
and
36 Golden Square, London W1R 4AH
866 United Nations Plaza, New York, NY 10017, USA
117 York Street, Sydney, NSW 2000, Australia
100 Skyway Avenue, Rexdale, Ontario, M9W 3A6, Canada
61 Beach Road, Auckland, New Zealand

Set, printed and bound in Great Britain by
Cox & Wyman Ltd, Reading
Set in Times

Granada ®
Granada Publishing ®

'Hate is the consequence of fear; we fear something before we hate it; a child who fears noises becomes a man who hates noise.'

Cyril Connolly, *The Unquiet Grave*

CHAPTER ONE

The shack was on the road between Pavlovsk and Pushkin, roughly fifteen miles from Leningrad. The sound of the guns was farther away now but they could hear machine-guns firing nearby, and smoke from the burning buildings filtered through the wounds of the wooden shack.

The young woman was twenty-two, but she looked middle-aged as she sat on the edge of the wooden planks covered with ragged clothes that they used as a bed. She sat holding the hand of the small boy whose neck was bandaged with a bloody shirt-sleeve. He was her son; his name was Yuri Galitsyn; and that day was his birthday. He was three years old, and he was quite still as they heard the screams and the shouting as they both watched the door. It fell from its worn leather hinges as the man's boot crashed it open. He stood there, a huge man in his torn and dusty Feldwebel's field-grey uniform, a machine-pistol hanging by its sling from his arm. He looked carefully round the room and as he took a step inside two other soldiers came in behind him.

He stood looking at the young woman and his big left hand reached forward, clutched at the centre of her ragged embroidered blouse and tore a great piece from its centre. He stood with the cloth in his clenched fist as he looked at her naked breasts. Then he said something to her that the boy couldn't understand. But he saw her nod and he saw the tears on her cheeks as she lay back on the bed.

The sergeant grinned and handed the machine-pistol to one of the others. And as the small boy stood holding his mother's hand the man unbuttoned his flies and got on top of her. The others had their turn and then they started again. It was an hour later when they had had enough. And all the time the little boy had held his mother's hand, silent and still. When they had finished the sergeant stood at the door

7

and as the girl groaned and leaned up on one elbow he raised his machine-pistol and the bullets sent wood splinters flying from the floor until her slight frame jerked as half a dozen slugs stitched across her body and she fell back silently on the layer of old clothes. As the grinning soldier swung his pistol towards the boy, a ball of fire from a flame-thrower enveloped the door of the wooden shack.

It was the 14th of July, 1941 and von Leeb's Army Group North were smashing their way north to take Leningrad.

CHAPTER TWO

He went into the station the second time through the entrance in Buckingham Palace Road and then walked up to the main concourse. There were two military policemen, a sergeant and a corporal checking the documents of a group of soldiers, but apart from these there were no police in evidence. He walked slowly through to the continental departure platforms. They still had the sign up for the Golden Arrow but the bookstall that sold Livres de Poche and Tauchnitz editions was closed.

At the main bookstall he bought a copy of the *Daily Mail*. The headline said 'Germans thrusting at Leningrad' and in the Stop Press it said that Berlin radio had been off the air. At the bottom of the page was an RAF advertisement for fighter pilots. He folded the paper and tucked it under his arm as he looked around. Then he walked across to the lockers and reached in his pocket for the key as he walked.

Locker 957 was towards the centre of the block, the second row down. As the metal door swung open he saw that it was there. It was so wide that they had had to put it diagonally from corner to corner. And it was very heavy as he pulled it out. He closed the locker door and threaded his way past the luggage trucks towards Platform 17 and showed his ticket for East Croydon.

He found an empty carriage but made no move to open the leather case. He sat quite still, except when from time to time he nervously touched the bulge at the right-hand side of his jacket caused by the documents and wallet in his inside pocket.

From East Croydon station he walked briskly to the old-fashioned terraced house that faced the railway sidings. He let himself in with his key and went up the stairs. He put down the case to unlock the door of his room, and once inside he put the case behind the curtain that screened off the lower part of the wash-basin.

He was lighting the gas burner to make himself some coffee when there was a knock on the door and he heard the landlady's voice say, 'Are you there, Mr Bailey? There's a gentleman downstairs to see you.'

There was a moment's silence before he said, 'Who is he? What does he want?'

'He's from the Employment Exchange.'

'I'll come down, Mrs Hardy.'

He heard her creaking down the stairs as he looked through his documents. He found it immediately and he put it inside the flap of his wallet. Opening the door he walked towards the stairs, and at the top he saw a man was already half-way up. A young man who looked up and nodded. 'Thought I'd save you the trouble, Mr Bailey. My, these stairs are steep.'

The man got to the top and said, 'Which is your room?'

Bailey said nothing but pointed to the furthest door and then walked ahead and opened the door.

The man from the Employment Exchange glanced briefly round the room and then, without any invitation, pulled out one of the bentwood chairs and sat down at the table.

'Where are you working, Mr Bailey?'

'I've only been here a day, I haven't got a job yet.'

'How old are you?'

'Twenty-three.'

'Why aren't you in the services?'

'I've got a spot on my lung. I'm C3. I've got a medical certificate.'

'Can I see it?'

Bailey opened his wallet, unfolded the paper and handed it to the man who looked at it carefully and then laid it on the table. He looked up at Bailey who was still standing.

'Where have you come from, Mr Bailey?'

'From Birmingham.'

'What was your address there?'

'Sixty-seven Quinton Road.'

'Bombed out were you?'

Bailey looked surprised. 'Yes. How did you know?'

The other man half-smiled, 'I guessed that's why you had moved up here.'

'That's right.'

'Have you got an identity card?'

'Yes, of course.'

The man held out his hand and Bailey sorted through his papers and then handed over the card. The man looked at it carefully for a couple of minutes, turning it over and checking both sides. Finally he laid that on top of the medical certificate and looked up at Bailey. For the first time Bailey was aware of the young man's hard, grey eyes.

'Sit down, Mr Bailey.'

Bailey pulled out a chair and sat down slowly.

'Where's the case?' The man said.

'What case?'

'The one you took from the locker at Victoria Station.'

'When was this?'

The man looked at his watch then back at Bailey's face. 'It was exactly forty-five minutes ago.'

'I've not been anywhere near Victoria Station.'

'We took a film of you, Mr Bailey. It will be processed by now. I'll show it to you some time.' And the man leaned back slightly in his chair and reached inside his jacket to bring out a folded identity card. He opened it and held it between his finger and thumb, so that it faced Bailey. Then he folded it and put it back in his inside pocket.

'Mr name is Boyle, Mr Bailey. Captain Boyle. And I am taking you into custody.'

Bailey's face was white, his hand on the table was trembling and he took a deep breath before he spoke.

'Why, what have I done?'

Boyle stood up, his eyes on Bailey's face. Some instinct told him to treat the man gently. He picked up the documents from the table.

'They didn't give you a sporting chance, Bailey. Did you know that?'

11

When Bailey made no answer Boyle put out his hand. 'Give me the key to this room and the house door.'

Bailey groped in his pocket and handed over the two keys.

When they were going down the stairs Bailey saw that there was another man standing in the tiny hallway. He was in battle-dress. A sergeant with green flashes on his arms, and a revolver in a webbing holster on his belt.

Boyle said, 'Book him in at Wandsworth. I'll be over in a couple of hours. No interrogation, but search him and take a tally of his stuff.'

The sergeant nodded and opened the front door of the house. The sunshine was bright and two or three people were standing on the far side of the road watching the police-car.

Boyle went back upstairs and searched the room thoroughly. He found the case under the wash-basin almost immediately. He placed it on the table-top upside down, and smoothed his fingers slowly over every part of it. He could feel none of those metal straps that often indicated a booby-trap. Turning the case over, he released the clasps and opened the lid.

There was a thin, fawn raincoat folded across the whole of the top. When that was lifted off he saw the radio. It was in two parts with a carefully packed tin of spares. A layer of shirts and underwear covered the two brown paperbags which held the money. There was £400 in one pound notes. Wrapped in a pair of dark blue woollen socks was the Morse-key and its connecting wires. Together with a razor and blades was a small bottle and a black-covered notebook. There was a bar of soap and a fountain-pen.

He checked the room twice but there was nothing. He carried the leather case to his car which was parked about fifty yards up the road. It was an MG with its hood down, and he put the case on the passenger seat. He sat there for two or three minutes, thinking, the engine running. Then he let in the clutch and drove off.

At Wandsworth Boyle registered everything that he had taken from Bailey and then telephoned a Whitehall number and asked for Colonel Parker. When Parker came on the telephone Boyle said quietly, 'I think I've got a suitable subject for the Twenty Committee.'

'Tell me.'

'Well for a start we've got him cold, the usual forged identity card, a forged medical certificate, a radio and £400. I have a hunch that he would co-operate.'

'Based on what?'

'I don't know, sir. Just the look of him. He's scared but there's still some spirit there.'

'What radio has he got?'

'It's a new one with provision for three crystals, but nothing very complicated.'

'Have Signals checked him yet?'

'No. I've only just booked him in.'

There was a long silence at the other end. Then Parker said, 'Pull him to pieces slowly. Charge him and soften him up a bit. See how you go.'

'What if he seems co-operative, sir?'

'Then contact me, I'll be at Broadway until late. If it goes over to tomorrow then you can get me at the Royal Thames.'

A Field Security sergeant brought Bailey into the interrogation room. It was plain concrete, white-washed and no windows. There was a small solid table in the centre of the room, its legs bolted to the floor. Boyle waved Bailey to the empty chair. That too was fixed to the floor.

Boyle leaned forward with his arms on the table and looked intently at Bailey's face. It was a full face with sensual lips, and the eyes were big and brown. His hair was black, and the waves at the front became curls at his neck. It was a weak face with a schoolboy pout, but Boyle guessed that it would be attractive to women.

'I hope you have had time to consider your position, Mr Bailey.'

The man licked his lips but said nothing. Boyle went on, 'Now let me inform you that your identity card is a very poor forgery. I am surprised that the Abwehr are still sacrificing you people by such carelessness.'

Boyle reached to the pile of Bailey's possessions on the table. He picked up the identity card and spread it out, turning it so that Bailey could see it the right way up.

'You see this code number. The four letters starting with Q are the code of the census officer. The next group of figures represents the electoral district in which the household was located. The second group of figures represents the electoral roll number of the family concerned, and finally, this last number. On your card it's thirty-seven. That number represents the position in the family of the person on the card. One for father, two for mother, three for eldest child, etcetera, etcetera. So according to your card your parents had at least thirty-five children. That's not very bright, is it, Mr Bailey?'

'Can I have a cigarette?'

'Later, maybe. Now on your card you'll see that it's folded twice. Beautifully machine-folded. But the genuine card is folded by its owner and they never do it so neatly. And the last thing is the surface of the card. Your forgery has what printers call a machine-finished surface. The real ones are matt and quite rough.'

Bailey still sat silently.

'Now we come to the address you gave me in Birmingham. As you well know, that house was bombed almost nine months ago. They told you that at your training school. They even showed you photographs. They said it was a safe address to give because nobody could check-up who had lived there. But unfortunately for you they gave that same address to six other agents. And that's very careless. It also means that we have checked that address very thoroughly. Everybody who lived in that house when it was bombed is accounted for. Two grandparents, a mother and two children were the only people who lived in that house when it was bombed. They were all killed and their bodies

14

were recovered. That address is only given to German agents who complete their training at the Abwehr Aussenstelle in Hamburg. The man who gave you your briefing was Hauptsturmführer Kuhrer. And he screws the blonde girl in the cyphers office. Is that enough?'

Bailey's face was white and he said, 'A cigarette. What about a cigarette?'

Boyle reached for the notepad and pencil and turned over to a fresh page.

'What's your real name?'

Bailey's hand was shaking as it went to his mouth. It was difficult to understand what he said.

'What happened to the six people?'

Boyle stood up and pushed back his chair with an angry look on his face.

'If you don't want to co-operate, Bailey, that's your problem, but I can't waste more time on you.'

'What happens?'

Boyle turned back to look at the German. 'We talk. And then I decide what happens.'

'You decide yourself?'

'Yes.'

'OK. I'll talk with you.'

Boyle walked back to the table and sat down. He took a packet of Goldflake and a lighter from his battle-dress pocket, pushed them across the table and waited for the other man to light up. There was a tin lid on the table as an ash-tray.

Boyle spoke softly. 'I must say you speak excellent English. Where'd you pick it up?'

'My mother was English, from Croydon.'

'Where did they drop you?'

'In Kent. On Romney Marshes.'

'Where on the marshes?'

'Near Appledore.'

'When was this?'

'Six days ago.'

'How did you get up here?'

15

'I got a car lift to Ashford station and then a train to Waterloo.'

'And you were trained at Hamburg?'

'Yes.'

'What were you doing when they recruited you?'

'I was a free-lance photographer. Sports and general stuff.'

'Why did they pick you up?'

'Black market.'

'Go on.'

'I sold nudes for cigarettes.'

'What's your real name?'

'Lemke. Otto Lemke.'

'Where were you born?'

'Brunswick.'

'What did they tell you to report on?'

'Weather, airfields, and aircraft production.'

'What grade radio operator were you when you finished?'

'Grade one.'

'Did they tell you what would happen if you were caught?'

'They said I would go to jail and to wait until they came over.'

Boyle smiled. 'If they gave you four hundred pounds you must have expected a long wait.'

Lemke shrugged. 'I had no choice.'

'When did you join the party?'

'I'm not a member.'

'What about party organizations?'

'Just Hitler Youth.'

'What do you want to do now, Lemke?'

'Have I got any choice?'

'Maybe. We'll see. When were you supposed to go on net?'

'As soon as possible.'

'Was there a Norwegian on your course?'

Lemke nodded.

'Was his name Per Heyerdahl?'

'Yes.'

Boyle stood up slowly, stretching his arms.

'You can keep the cigarettes and the lighter, I'll tell the guards.'

'What will happen to me?'

'I'll see you tomorrow and we'll have another talk. The Signals people will be having a chat with you about your radio.'

Lemke nodded, and the big brown eyes watched Boyle as he left the room.

Boyle sat alone in the small outer office and checked through Lemke's belongings. Technical Facilities had already identified the leather wallet as of German manufacture. It was a light brown suede, expensive and hand-made. There were eighteen one-pound notes, the identity card and the medical certificate. And Boyle sighed as he shook out the papers from the deep inside pocket. The Abwehr people at Hamburg were so stupid. There was the torn half of a night-club cloak-room ticket with a Hamburg telephone number, a photograph of a middle-aged woman with a dog and on the reverse side was the Agfa trade-mark. Facilities had already put in a request for the wallet so that it could be passed to SOE for their agents' use. The last item was a condom in a paper envelope. It was the first time that Boyle had discovered such a sign of optimism in an agent's kit.

He looked at his watch. It was just on midnight and he decided to leave phoning Parker until the next day.

CHAPTER THREE

Parker sat, filling the club chair, looking up at the ornate plaster work on the ceiling. Without looking down he said, 'Changing the subject, when are you seeing your father again?'

'I hoped I might see him this afternoon, sir.'

'He's still down in Limpsfield?'

'Yes. I don't think he'll ever move. And it's handy for town.'

'And your mother?'

'She's fine apart from her asthma.'

'Good. Now back to our friend Lemke. You say Signals are satisfied about the safety checks and the rest of it.'

'Yes.'

'I had a word with The Twenty Committee liaison man. They're keen, but they're thin on the ground for bodies.' Parker shoved himself upright in the chair. 'They asked if you could be spared as controller for Lemke. What do you think?'

'I'd rather not, sir.'

'Why not?'

'It's not my line, sir. I'm Intelligence Corps not Signals.'

Parker was fiddling with a shoe-lace as he spoke. '*All* the controllers are I Corps. The Signals people work with them.'

Boyle sighed. 'Whatever you say, sir.'

'Fine. I'll have it put through Part II orders.'

Otto Lemke looked as though he hadn't slept for a week. His eyes were half-closed and a nerve quivered below one eye. He shifted uneasily in the interrogation chair as Boyle sorted out his notes.

'Tell me again about your father, Otto.'

'Like I said, I don't remember anything really. He went off when I was four or five.'

'And your mother?'

'She was very pretty. I think she liked me but she hadn't got much time so she had to leave me with people while she earned money.'

'You said you weren't sure what she did for a living.'

Boyle looked at Lemke's face as he asked him the question. Lemke looked away towards the door, and then back to look down at his hands.

'I suppose when you get down to it she was a tart.' He looked up at Boyle's face. 'But she was a jolly woman. Everybody was always laughing when she was around. And she always bought me things before she went off again.'

'When did you go back to Germany?'

'About thirty-five. My father asked her to go back.'

'How did it work out?'

Lemke shrugged. 'He wasn't there when we arrived but she found a man and we lived with him.'

'How old were you when you left home?'

'I left straightaway. I was seventeen.'

'And you worked for a local newspaper in Hanover?'

'I did all sorts of jobs. Anything that paid money.'

'When they suggested that you work for the Abwehr what was your reaction?'

'I said OK. They said they'd drop the charges and that I'd be trained. They paid me well and looked after me.'

'You said that you sold nude photographs for black market cigarettes?'

'Yes.'

'It was a bit more than that, wasn't it?'

'What makes you think that?'

'Because I know how the Abwehr recruit people to work for them.'

Boyle noticed the angry defensive look on Lemke's face and he said softly, 'Would you rather *I* told *you*?'

Lemke nodded.

'I think you pimped for a girl. Yes?'

'That's what *they* called it. She lived with me and we needed the money. She didn't go with just anybody. They were men I got to know. More like friends really. One of them told me he was a government clerk. He was really a clerk in the Abwehr office in Langestrasse, and when he found out I was bilingual in English he reported it to them. The girl was just an excuse. They would have found some excuse or other to pull me in.'

'How did they treat you?'

'Not bad. I had to live at the building. But it was interesting, the training. And I reckoned it would give me protection; and the radio stuff would be useful when the war is over.'

'When d'you think that will be?'

Lemke grinned. 'God knows. They said before Christmas.'

'What do *you* think?'

'Depends on what the Americans do.'

'What's your radio security check-word?'

Lemke sighed. '*Recht.*'

'And the second check-word?'

'*Unter.*'

'My Signals people say that you co-operated sensibly with them.'

The young German shrugged. 'I don't have any choice.'

'You look as though you haven't been sleeping. Are you worried?'

'What's going to happen to me?'

'That depends on you.'

'In what way?'

'You're an enemy agent, Otto. Forged documents, radio and all that. The penalty on both sides is execution. I shall recommend that because you have co-operated that you are merely imprisoned.'

Lemke nodded. 'I hoped it would help.'

'We could go further than that if you wanted to.'

Lemke looked at Boyle's face and whispered. 'They could find out. They'd have me killed.'

'They haven't found out about the others.'

'You mean you're using Abwehr people.'

'Yes.'

'What would I have to do?'

'Just send the messages we give you.'

'What happens if the Germans invade?'

'The records would be destroyed and you would be given new documents and a passage to Canada by air. They'll find you a job over there.'

'Where would I be transmitting from?'

'For a month you would be transmitting from here. If that went satisfactorily you would live as a civilian with your controlling officer.'

'Who would that be?'

'Me.'

Lemke closed his eyes for a moment as he thought, then, opening his eyes and shrugging, he said, 'OK. I'll do it.'

For two weeks Lemke transmitted from his cell in the interrogation centre the short innocuous messages that the 'double-cross' staff had worked out to establish a plausible 'cover' for the German. To his masters in Hamburg he was now a traveller for a company manufacturing office stationery. His medical history and forged documents gave him a medical status of C3 which made him a much sought-after employee by many companies whose staff had left for the services. And the fresh-air, out-door life of a travelling salesman would not only alleviate his supposed medical condition but provide easy opportunities for visiting towns and villages in the south-east that could supply the information that the Aussenstelle in Hamburg required.

By the fourth week he was able to identify for them the army units guarding the perimeter of Biggin Hill and the name of a pub at Brasted used every night by the fighter pilots not on duty. In the middle of week six Lemke moved with Boyle to a cottage on Limpsfield Chart. They were joined by a Royal Corps of Signals sergeant and an ATS girl in civilian clothes who was a corporal in Signals Security. A middle-aged Scotswoman named Mrs Maclean acted as housekeeper to them all. By the second month they settled into a routine that was almost untouched by the real war.

There were three hours to go before Lemke's next transmission schedule and Boyle had cycled the two miles downhill to Limpsfield village and his home.

'The Sheiling' stood back from the road in four acres mainly given over to landscaped park, but in the south-east corner a coppice of beech and oak marked the edge of the church's glebe land. The house itself was an L-shaped structure of stone with its original mullioned windows and lead rain-water pipes with a thistle moulded on their heads. It had been the Boyle home for three hundred years and neither the present incumbent nor any of his predecessors had ever felt any need to alter its external structure.

Andrew Boyle stood watching his son lodge his cycle against the low wall that separated the rose garden from the sweep of the lawns in front of the house. Andrew Boyle would not have admitted, even to himself, to being pleased with the kind of man his son had developed into. Satisfied is the word he would have chosen. If you were the senior partner in a firm of solicitors that had handled the affairs of a good many of the families of wealth and influence for a century and a half, you were not given to hasty judgements, however consoling they might be.

Despite their Scottish roots the Boyles had always practised their law in England, and young James Boyle had kept his terms at Lincoln's Inn until the outbreak of war. It could have easily been arranged for his military service to be deferred for the nine months necessary to complete his admission but he had volunteered on the 4th September, 1939. He had been commissioned directly into the Intelligence Corps and had been made responsible for assisting with the assessment of appeals by suspect aliens arrested under Regulation 18b in the first weeks of the war. By the time France fell he was deputy liaison officer between MI5 and the Joint Intelligence Committee. On the advice of one of

22

his seniors he had grown a moustache to camouflage his youth. He was twenty-one.

The two of them sat on the lawn sipping whisky in silence as they watched the blackbirds listening for worms. The silence was broken when a woman with red hair walked over to them. Both men stood up as she approached them.

'Well,' she said, 'what are you two up to.'

James Boyle smiled. 'Sit down, mother.'

'No I won't just now. I've got some of my ladies in the house. They won't be more than half an hour. Can you stay for supper, Jimmy?'

'Yes. If it's convenient.'

She laughed softly. 'One of these days one of you two is going to do something wild in public. All this restraint can't last. I hope I'm around to see it.'

And still smiling at her thoughts she turned away and walked slowly back to the house.

Andrew Boyle looked over the top of his glass as he sipped his whisky.

'There's gossip in the village about your place up on the Chart.'

'What are they saying?'

'Oh, like a jury, they're right in their instincts but wrong in the solution. You're a nest of German spies signalling to the German planes to help them on their way to London. But they're sure that the police have got their eye on you.'

'What's all that based on?'

The older man watched his son's face to see if it registered the main point.

'You're spies because you don't buy food in the village. And you don't do that because you haven't got ration books. And Constable Pickering has been seen at the cottage twice.'

'I suppose somebody will report us soon.'

'I doubt it.'

'Why?'

Boyle senior smiled. 'As I said, they think you're waving the planes on to London and that makes you no worse than the brigands down on the marshes who used to lure Spanish galleons on to the rocks with their lanterns.'

'I'd better ask Parker to speak to the Chief Constable.'

'Parker's coming down here tomorrow, I could ask the Chief Constable over for a drink if he wants.'

'Thanks. I'll ask him.'

'How do you find Parker?'

'Dedicated. Thinks of nothing but winning the war.'

He had sat with Lemke and the Signals sergeant while Lemke tapped out the coded message to Hamburg, and waited while Lemke took down their return traffic.

After Lemke had left with the sergeant, Boyle had sat for a few moments looking at the message pad. The knock at the door had startled him.

'Come in.'

It was the ATS girl.

'Could I have a word with you, sir?'

'By all means. Do sit down.'

She was about twenty-four. A pretty girl. A twin sets and pearls sort of girl. The kind of girl that the Intelligence services tended to recruit. She made herself comfortable and then looked at him.

'This is a bit awkward, sir. But I thought I'd better mention it to you. It's about Lemke.'

She waited as if she needed his permission and he nodded, 'Go on please.'

'I think you ought to get him a girl, sir.'

'Why is that, Miss er . . . I'm sorry.'

'That's all right – it's Angela Tredgold.'

'Why should we get him a girl?'

'The usual reason, sir. He's a randy sod.'

Boyle was as startled as if he had been struck. He had never heard such words from a girl, and could barely believe that an upper-class girl could even know the meaning of what she was saying.

'How do you know all this.'

'He's been chasing me round the furniture for two weeks,

24

sir. Says he hasn't had a woman for three months. He's built up quite a head of steam, sir.'

Boyle was on the point of saying that he hadn't had a woman in his whole life but abandoned it as not being relevant. 'I'm terribly sorry. I'll speak to him first thing in the morning. We'll soon put a stop to that.'

'You'd be wasting your time, sir. He needs a girl. Some men are like that,' she said, to soften the blow.

'I hope you weren't scared too badly.'

'Good grief no. I knew he'd get me in a corner sooner or later.'

'You mean he actually assaulted you.'

'I wouldn't put it quite like that, sir. We compromised.'

And as the implications of the words sank in he looked back at her face. She was smiling. And he realized that she hadn't minded what had happened and he felt a spasm of lust as he became aware of her body.

'Well,' he said, 'thanks for putting me in the picture. I'll have to work something out.'

And then she was gone, and he sat there thinking of what she had said. He wondered if the compromise had been what he thought it had been, and for a few vertiginous moments he imagined what it would have been like if he had been the man. Then he shook his head to dismiss the thought and stood up. But as he undressed he felt anger that a crude man like Lemke could imagine that a girl like that would satisfy his lust. But the vision became erotic. He guessed what the girl had done, but his mind wandered over what the girl might have let Lemke do to her, and for a few moments his mind was flooded with thoughts of the girl's breasts and legs and the warm softness of her body. He switched off the light and stood in the darkness until his lust abated.

The following morning he spoke to Parker who indicated neither surprise nor dislike for Lemke's needs, and merely told him that he would send down some photographs so that Lemke could make his own choice. And then he passed on to Fighter Command's interest in the Abwehr's change of

25

direction in information required from Lemke regarding the control centre at Rye.

When the envelope of photographs arrived by dispatch rider he left the envelope unopened.

He raised the subject with Lemke when they were walking on the Chart that afternoon. He found a massive felled beech for them to sit on. He was determined to treat the matter as a piece of routine. Something that he had to do as part of his duties.

'I understand,' he started, 'that you'd like us to find you a girlfriend, Otto.'

The German was looking down the leafy drive between the trees and he turned quickly to look at Boyle.

'Maybe they'd let us both go up to London for a night.'

'That won't be necessary. I've got some photographs here. You might like to pick one.' And he handed Lemke the still unopened envelope. The German ripped it open clumsily and looked slowly through the eight or nine photographs. Sometimes turning back to look at one of them a second time. Finally he went back to the second photograph and handed it to Boyle.

'How much would that one cost me?'

Boyle ignored the photograph.

'It won't cost you anything. She will be provided.'

Lemke's face lit up. 'That's fantastic. She'll stay with us, will she?'

'If that's what you want.'

'Yes. That's fantastic. Thanks.'

Boyle took the other photographs and slid them all back in the envelope. They walked for a couple of miles and then circled back to the cottage.

Boyle sat with Lemke that evening checking the coding of the evening's transmission. He checked it three times and then passed it to the Signals sergeant who took it to the small radio room to await transmission time. It covered damage done to the Dover–Canterbury railway-lines in a Luftwaffe raid three weeks earlier. The information given

26

was brief but true, and Boyle had taken Lemke down to see the damage so that he could compose a message in his own style which London Control would clear with every authority's 'double-cross' liaison officer. The name 'double-cross' committee had been converted in the early days to the more subtle 'XX Committee' and finally 'The Twenty Committee' for the sake of security. There were almost forty German agents whose radios were working back to Germany under the control of British Intelligence. The elaborate game was master-minded by men whose knowledge of the enemy was prodigious, and each piece of the jig-saw supplied by one turned operator had to fit the total picture that would emerge in the RSHA centre in Berlin. It took longer to clear a piece of false information than to clear one based on fact, because real suspicion at the other end could bring down the whole web of deceit. Some day *all* the messages would be false, and that could save a million lives, but until that day the controls were painstaking and rigid.

After eating alone in his room that evening Boyle looked at the photographs. The girls were all dressed, but in such a way that their breasts and legs were clearly defined. The caption on the back of the photograph of the girl Lemke had chosen said simply: 'Mary Pierce – aged eighteen.' He passed the print number to Parker who told him to keep the photographs until the next messenger came. The girl would be sent down as soon as possible.

The transmission that night had been abortive. There had been no response on either frequency from Hamburg. Not even an acknowledgement that Lemke's transmission had been received. The procedure laid down by the Abwehr meant no transmissions for the next two nights.

CHAPTER FOUR

Boyle was down at his father's house when the girl arrived but he saw her when he got back. She was very pretty with long black hair and big grey eyes, and she looked even younger than the eighteen claimed on the caption. His eyes went to her full breasts, and when he looked back at her face she had been smiling. An amused smile that seemed to accept men's interest in her body as being normal and acceptable. He found little to say to her and went straight to his room at the back of the cottage.

It had been four days before Hamburg came back on the network. There were no explanations but they asked Lemke to repeat his previous two messages.

It was almost three months later. The night of December the 8th. The night of Pearl Harbor. The girl came into his room as he was undressing. She was wearing only her skirt and her face was white and frightened.

'He says he's gonna kill himself.'

'Who does?'

'Otto. He heard the news about the Japs. He's scared.'

'Stay here till I come back.'

Lemke was sitting on the edge of the bed his face in his hands, rocking up and down in a frenzy of fear. Boyle reached out, and gripping one wrist he put his hand under Lemke's chin, forcing it up so that he looked at him. The German's eyes were red with weeping and his face was wet with tears. He trembled as Boyle looked at him in silence.

'Tell me what's upset you, Otto.'

'The Japs, by God. You've lost the war now. This is it. They'll kill me. I was crazy to do it. You forced me you know. It wasn't ...'

And he vomited a stinking mess of beer and food that

28

flooded warm over Boyle's arm. But it seemed to calm him, and Boyle spoke quietly and slowly without taking away his hands.

'Roosevelt has already declared war on Germany as well as Japan. It's the beginning of the end for the Nazis, Otto. They don't stand a chance. Russia, the United States and the British Empire . . . it's just a matter of time.'

Lemke shook his head. He was shivering as if he had a fever.

'They'll kill me. They'll kill me like a dog.'

'Otto Lemke, you've got five hundred million people fighting on your side.'

The German's shivering was subsiding and there were two red spots of colour on his drawn cheeks.

'I made a mistake, Captain. I should have gone to jail.'

Boyle sat down facing him on the wicker chair.

'Otto. They don't suspect you. I can get you back to Germany right now through Lisbon, or Madrid, if that's what you want. We'll pay you for what you've already done. And they'll give you a hero's welcome.'

Lemke's large brown eyes stared at his face, and he said softly, 'D'you mean that?'

'Of course I mean it.'

Lemke breathed deeply, very slowly, as if he were exercising his lungs. Then again, and a third time. And a few moments later he grinned at Boyle.

'It scared me hearing that. They sank half the American fleet. It's fantastic.'

'It was crazy. The Americans are ready to go. They'll smash the Nazis first and then the Japs.'

'How long before it's over?'

'Two years, maybe three. And month by month you'll see them put through the wringer. There'll be some set-backs but it's just a question of time now.'

'You got a whisky for me, Cap'n?'

'No. You need some sleep. I'll give you a shot to make you sleep, and you'll be bright and shiny tomorrow morning. Just lie back and I'll be with you.'

He was back with the syringe a couple of minutes later and he pinched up a vein on Lemke's left arm, sterilized the area, and slid in the needle. He pressed the plunger slowly and evenly.

Lemke lay with his eyes closed and a few minutes later he was breathing deeply. Boyle closed and locked the door behind him but he guessed that Lemke would be out for at least ten hours.

When he went back in his room Boyle poured himself a whisky before he remembered the girl. He turned to look for her. She was sitting on his bed watching him with anxious eyes.

'He's all right now,' he said. 'Would you like a whisky?'

She nodded, and he poured her a drink and handed it to her. He looked at her naked breasts and she moved the glass away so that his view was unobstructed. And as he looked she said, 'What's Otto doing?'

'He's asleep. I gave him a shot of morphine. He'll be OK tomorrow.'

'You like me to sleep in here tonight?'

He looked at her face without answering, and she said, 'You want me, don't you?'

'What makes you say that?'

She smiled. 'I've seen the way you look at me sometimes when you come into Otto's room. And Otto says you're not a homo.'

She lay back on the bed and patted the space alongside her. The next day all that he could remember was the yielding softness of her breasts, and her body responding to his. He knew that he had had her again and again, with a silent animal lust. But it had been in some other world. A world without inhibitions, a world of soft girl-flesh and incredible sensations. He had slept until mid-morning and when he awoke he thanked God that he was alone.

The girl smiled at him when they met later that day in Lemke's room. And when Lemke left them alone to get cigarettes she said softly, smiling, 'Was it good?'

30

He avoided the question and said, 'You're beautiful, Mary. Very beautiful.'

And when he stood up to leave she said, 'You can do that any time you want.'

He left the room without speaking.

As the months passed Lemke's role became more and more important, and in the month before D-Day the Germans wanted more and more information about military units. They no longer asked for information about airfields or anti-aircraft sites. Information was fed back piece by piece, and now more than half of it was false. Units were identified that had never existed, and special signals units were formed which did nothing but create signals traffic to and from these imaginary divisions.

Lemke had long ago forgotten his doubts and fears but he still seemed temperamentally and psychologically dependent on Boyle. There had been half a dozen different girls and Lemke was only interested in teenagers. Two months after D-Day Boyle's operation was closed down, but the security net was still as tight as it had ever been. There was just the housekeeper, Boyle and Lemke, and his latest girl, a seventeen-year-old from Cardiff, several years his junior, with a schoolgirl innocence on her face that was entirely deceptive.

Lemke was given the choice of Canada, Britain or occupied Germany for his post-war home, and he finally decided that it would be Germany. After the Germans' push in the Ardennes had been crushed, Lemke was posted as a German civilian to a Military Government detachment that would control the Göttingen area in the extreme south of the British zone. He was given new documents, a de-nazification certificate and three thousand pounds in newly-minted sovereigns.

For his last two weeks in England he stayed in a luxury flat in St James's with Boyle, and there were virtually no more security restrictions. There were shopping expeditions for clothes and a constant stream of girls until the day that

Boyle drove him down to Hurn Airport outside Bournemouth and saw him on to the Dakota that would take him to Hanover.

For a month or two there was a flow of letters but they gradually tapered off to silence. There were Christmas cards for a few years and that was the end of it all.

Boyle was admitted to the Bar in 1947 and had joined a busy chambers in Lincoln's Inn. The head of the chambers was an old friend of his father, who then made it a point of honour to cease using those chambers for any of his work.

In the Soviet Union Yuri Galitsyn was seven years old when the war ended. His only clothing was a canvas sack tied round his skinny waist with an artilleryman's lanyard. Still visible on the sack were the stencil marks of the sugar plant at Smolensk. His head was shaven to the skin, but even in that minute stubble the head lice still laid their eggs. One arm and one hand, fortunately the left, were an angry purple where the flame-thrower had caught him. Although that had been four years ago the skin still erupted from time to time so that it ran wet with a kind of dew. Sometimes, if the unit that had adopted him was near a town, a doctor or a vet would cover the limb in the stockholm tar that they used on sick animals at the collectives.

At the end of 1946 the artillery unit was posted to Berlin and the small boy was sent to a transit camp for unclaimed children. There were 90,000 children in the camp, and there were 102 similar camps which together held one and a half million children under the age of fourteen. No administration in the world could have done anything more than provide an existence for the children. They were kept in the camps for two years. Waiting, like the strays in a dogs' home, to be claimed. When, at the end of the two years, there had been no claimants the children were sent in groups of two hundred or so to the State orphanages in Siberia. Not as a punishment, but in a country almost completely destroyed on its western marches, the cold beyond the Urals was the only area where some sort of administration still functioned, and where there were buildings that could be converted into workable orphanages.

The children themselves were not easy to control with their temperaments ranging from a stunned lethargy to manic resentment of all authority. And as background there was a government and nation in turmoil, exhausted by its sacrifices, secretly only half-believing in its victories, fearful and suspicious of its allies and the future; its main concern to build a wall a hundred miles deep around its frontiers to ensure that the nightmare could never happen again.

Yuri Galitsyn had seen and absorbed the soldiers' discipline, and by the time he was ten he was already respected by his fellows and the teachers and staff at the orphanage. He was bright and energetic, and they marked him down as first-rate material for one of the military academies.

There was still an eerie silence all over Europe, as if the people were holding their breath, listening for news of their fate, now that peace had come.

CHAPTER FIVE

There was a smell of paint hanging over the courtroom from the decorating going on in the corridors, and as counsel for the Director of Public Prosecutions opened his reference at the second tagged page Mr Justice Laker moved his arm so that he could surreptitiously look at his watch. It was barely three o'clock and he had had hopes of adjourning no later than four. But by the time counsel had made his point on the interpretation of Section Two of the Official Secrets Act it would be well after half past three. And although defending counsel would not say so the court would be well aware that to adjourn without the response being established could be construed as unfair. On the grounds that juries could not retain the subtle points of law overnight without prejudice to the defence case.

As he watched Boyle press flat the pages of his reference book he wondered if Boyle were not still a bit too young to be offered a judgeship. He was sound enough, but in the criminal courts the public was beginning to take against the prosecutors and prefer the defenders. A logical reaction to the massive pressure of more and more offences created by government after government. And James Boyle, QC, had been a prosecutor for most of his thirty years at the Bar. He had a prosecutor's face. Lean and lined, the skin tight over the bony structure, and eyes that were penetrating, even across a court. And he had a prosecutor's manner; self-assured, dominating, perhaps even domineering. But Boyle took nothing for granted, every facet of a Boyle presentation was well-nigh perfect. Every defence move anticipated, and the appropriate counter-argument marshalled and ready. He was neither popular nor unpopular with his Bar colleagues, he was more an institution than a man. His whole life entirely devoted to the law. A game of golf from time to time was his only diversion; although he was willing to speak at influential gatherings so long as the subject allowed him to emphasize the importance of law and order.

When he had given the Reith Lectures his theme had been the confusion in the public's mind between justice and fairness. A confusion which Boyle claimed could so dilute the laws of the land that they became subject to the pressure of politicians, trade unions and what he referred to obliquely as 'syndicalists'. There were few on the Bench who disagreed with him, but there were politically appointed law-officers to whom he was anathema. The personification of implacable adherence to the letter of the law rather than its spirit. There had been a much publicized television discussion programme when a newly appointed Attorney-General had said as much. Boyle's skull-like head had turned, and the camera had caught the curve of contempt on his mouth as he said, 'There *is* only the letter of the law. Parliament writes the letter of the law; the judiciary merely apply those laws. There is no such thing as the spirit of the law, the phrase is only invoked by those who would like the judiciary to bend to their pressures to ignore the law when it suits them.' The repercussions had filled *The Times* letter columns for weeks.

Mr Justice Laker picked up his pencil as Boyle raised his head, and he wrote on his pad, 'Regina *v* Markham and others'. He nodded to Boyle that he was ready, and rested his jaw on one hand.

'Milord, my learned friend referred to the judgement of Lord Justice Salmon in the case of Regina *v* Parsons, and I should like to draw the court's attention to Lord Parker's comment on appeal of that same case; and in addition, to Lord Widgery's determination on conspiracy in Regina *v* Markham and others.'

Boyle waited while the Clerk of the Court handed up the open copy to the judge, who went through the motions of checking the page number and then nodded.

'Carry on, Mr Boyle.'

Boyle read the two references in his clipped Scots accent and when he had finished it was 3.35 p.m.

Mr Justice Laker read on for a few moments, and then put the heavy book on one side as he looked at his watch.

'I had had in mind going on to about four-thirty so that Sir Peter could establish his rebuttal. However, I sense that you will have other points you wish to lay before the court. How long will you need, Mr Boyle?'

'Forty-five minutes, milord.'

'Yes. I thought so. Well in that case I propose that we adjourn now until ten o'clock tomorrow, and you can complete your material and then I can hear the defence. Can I take it that you are both in agreement on this?'

Both men nodded and gave their assent, and the court adjourned.

In the corridor Boyle was stopped by one of the court reporters.

'Could I ask you a question, Mr Boyle.'

'Provided it's not about this case you may.'

'There's a rumour that the Lord Chancellor has offered you a judgeship. Could you confirm that.'

'Mr Craddock ... it is Mr Craddock, isn't it? I am sure that your editor would not expect me to comment on rumours.'

'If it were true, sir, would you accept?'

'If it were true, Mr Craddock, we should not be talking about rumours. Now I must be off.'

And his junior winked at the reporters as he fell in behind his master and headed for the stairs.

Boyle sat at the big mahogany table that his chambers had bought him for his fiftieth birthday. There were briefs piled up on a low table alongside his chair but the top of his table was bare except for a green blotter and a gold fountain-pen. And a letter. It lay there, its double folds making a triangle that hid the words at its centre.

For the hundredth time he picked up the thick white sheet and folded it open. There was the magnificent crest of the Lord Chancellor's office and the long flowing signature of the Lord Chancellor himself. The text was brief. Only four lines in all. He was offered a judgeship, to start in the next session. After the long recess.

His income from the law would go down by ten or fifteen thousand a year, but he had the income from his father's estate, the house at Limpsfield, and the small flat in Sloane Street. Most of it went in tax, and there was only himself to consider. No wife and no family, thank God. It was a straight decision ... did he want to be a judge or not. There had been those who could not afford to give up their Bar income, or who, in accepting, had made a big sacrifice. And there were those whose outgoing way of life as barristers was too attractive to be given up; and even some who needed the spur of winning and losing to make their lives worthwhile. There were not many who declined, and none who did it without regret. There were few enough who were given the chance. It was an accolade, not a reward.

Boyle's mother had died in 1950 after a long illness that had left his father a different man. Lethargic and absent-minded, no longer interested in the law-practice he sold out to the two junior partners, and lived the life of a recluse in the house at Limpsfield. At week-ends Boyle would go down late on a Friday night, and perhaps for an hour the older man's eyes would come alive, and he would take an interest in hearing the gossip of the courts. But he would slowly sink back into the mists that seemed for ever to swirl in his mind. The family doctor had told Boyle that his father had refused the drugs he prescribed to counter the depression. The housekeeper telephoned Boyle in his chambers from time to time when his father seemed to be particularly disturbed. And Boyle would travel down to find his father lying fully clothed on his bed, the curtains drawn, his eyes wide-open, staring at the ceiling. He would sit on the edge of the bed holding his father's hand as the old man talked slowly and haltingly to the woman who was long since dead. It seemed to Boyle a poor reward for a lifetime's love and devotion. He saw it as a grim warning to himself.

From time to time the old man had wandered from the house and the police brought him back. Eventually Boyle had gone back to the house each evening, and travelled to town each morning on the early train. And on summer evenings the old man had walked with him in the gardens, his thin hand holding his son's arm without knowing whose arm it was.

On the 1st of September the housekeeper had been waiting for him at the small country station. His father had died sitting in the garden half an hour earlier; and two men from the village had carried him upstairs to his bedroom where he lay, still holding a chestnut leaf in one hand. Even then there was no peace on the old man's face.

As the briefs that Boyle handled grew in importance, and when his success began to be a talking-point, he had received all those invitations that eligible bachelors can expect. For almost three years society hostesses had done their best with permutations of partners that ranged through the whole gamut from intellectuals to the scatter-brained, from classical beauties to the merely pretty. At thirty-seven, with a successful Bar practice, about to take silk, a splendid country home and no commitments, James Boyle was a very desirable property. His reputation for aloofness seemed barely credible when set against the charm and courtesy that were unfailingly available to all his partners. And if there *was* aloofness then all the more reason for a young woman to show that she was the one to lead him out of that ivory tower. But liquid brown eyes and the deepest of cleavages led to no more than kissed hands and a small bouquet the next morning.

There had been a girl. A girl from the village who came at week-ends when the housekeeper took her day off. She was young and pretty, and her smile reminded him of Lemke's girls. The third time she had come to the house she had prepared his strawberry tea for him in the kitchen and she had washed up while he ate, and told him the gossip of the village. A saga of babies and jobs, and unrequited loves. She had lingered until the light began to go, and the shadowy dusk had seemed to make it easy and natural when he took her upstairs. She had chattered away even as he undressed

38

her, and when she was naked she had lain complaisantly as
he made love to her. When it was over she had sat up,
stretching her arms as if she had been asleep, still talking her
innocent twaddle as she slowly dressed.

For a couple of months after this relationship had started
he had actually enjoyed the society dinners that he attended
during the week. Suddenly his life seemed to have achieved
some kind of balance. The stimulating, witty company in
town became more tolerable because of the week-end en-
counters. The men wondered what had come over their ascetic companion, and the ladies, in their wisdom,
conjectured on who the lucky lady might be. Much intimate
intelligence was passed back and forth, but without result.

When Boyle was with the girl he listened to her chatter as
he listened to music that he didn't understand; with mild
pleasure, but without involvement. She made no demands
on his mind and seemed contented to have him solely as an
audience. But he learned more about what really went on in
the village than he'd learned in all the years he had lived
there.

The London social scene had slackened during the
summer as families and couples moved out of town. It was
during this time that he made the two mistakes. He had
bought the girl a wrist-watch, not wildly expensive, but expensive enough. And without thinking that it could be
unwise, he had taken her to Brighton for a meal. No overnight stay, no hand-holding in public, because they never
did hold hands. Just a quiet meal to accompany her commentary on Mrs Salter's curtain-making, why the milkman
had a black-eye, and why the rams were put in with the ewes
on Guy Fawkes' night. He had delivered her back to the
village before 11 p.m.

It had not been until midday on the following Saturday
that he had noticed the housekeeper's silence and had asked
her what was the matter. Avoiding his eyes she had reached
into the pocket of her apron and put a small tissue-paper-
wrapped object on the table. When he had opened it it was
the wrist-watch, and the woman had said, 'Joe Greenaway

says she ain't to come no more.' He saw from her eyes, and heard from her voice, that she was in full agreement with Joe Greenaway. He had made no comment.

The first week in September he had gone to town for the retirement presentation to one of the High Court Registrars, and walking back to the taxi rank with a solicitor acquaintance he had been asked with a half-smile who the girl was he had taken to Brighton. He had pretended ignorance, and implied mistaken identity; but he knew it hadn't washed. There had been knowing half-smiles at dinner parties, and fewer invitations. Without conscious decision he accepted very few of the invitations which were proffered.

Despite the analytical mind that he applied to the rest of his life he avoided any analysis of his new situation. He vaguely wondered why he had never felt lust for the society girls, and he knew that there could be no sense in thinking of marriage with the girl from the village. Perhaps subconsciously he may have equated love with marriage, and marriage with his father's suffering when left alone. But love wasn't a word that was often in his thoughts. He only tolerated the brittle society girls; and he knew now that it wasn't possible to have that uncommitted rustic dream with village girls no matter what the village. The law would be mistress and wife for him. He must never again risk the humiliation that both sides of his social life had inflicted on him. It had seemed almost as if he were at their mercy, waiting anxiously for a favourable verdict. To hell with them all. He had been a fool, and once was enough for that.

Despite its soft bell he had been startled when his telephone rang.

'Boyle.'

'Mathews, sir. There's a Mr Parker would like a word with you.'

'Parker? Who is he?'

'Just a moment, sir. I'll check.'

Boyle sighed with impatience as he waited, and then Mathews was back again.

'Mr Parker says it's a personal call. Says you worked together during the war.'

'Ah yes. Of course. Put him through will you.'

There were the usual clicks, and then he heard that once familiar voice.

'Is that James Boyle?'

'Yes, sir. It's nice to hear from you. What are you doing these days?'

'I'm retired. Live not far from your place in Surrey. Just down the road at Dorking.'

'We must get together for a meal.'

'Well that's exactly what I called about. I was wondering if we could have dinner together quite soon?'

'When had you in mind?'

'Would it be possible this evening? At the Reform, perhaps.'

'Too political for me I'm afraid. How about the Travellers? About eight if that would suit you.'

'That would be excellent. I'll see you at eight, then.'

Boyle wondered what it could be. Maybe some regimental thing, but the Intelligence Corps wasn't much given to social occasions. But Parker wasn't the kind who would invite him to dinner hoping for free legal advice. He could recognize those by now a mile off. Anyway, whatever it was, Parker deserved a couple of hours of his time.

The events that brought the two men together again after thirty years had started over a month before when a television crew from NBC in New York had gone to East Berlin to film a documentary on the training of the East German girl gymnasts.

On the final day an East German journalist named Oskar Müller had given one of the cameramen an address in Pankow and asked him to pass it to the CIA so that they could contact him.

The TV team had been well briefed before they crossed into East Berlin and the cameraman had been non-committal. They had been warned specifically about such approaches. But the address and the message were passed on through one of the US Army Press officers at their Berlin HQ. It was with one of the CIA detachments a couple of hours later.

The CIA had contacted one of their people, an undertaker in Heinersdorf. He reported later that the address was a small newspaper and tobacco shop that made money on the side by renting its two small upstairs rooms by the hour for the benefit of impatient lovers and semi-professional amateurs. They had then used one of their men in the Volkspolizei to make the contact.

The shopkeeper had phoned a number and then shown the man upstairs. Twenty minutes later Oskar Müller had arrived. There had been the minimum of preliminaries and then Müller had said that he wanted to come over to the West. He had information to offer of the highest importance in return for American citizenship and a pension. He had suggested a crude code that could be used for messages, based on the German/English volume of *Langenscheidt*.

They had taken two days out to check on him, but apart from his genuine role as a respected free-lance sports journalist there was very little. He was married with a grown-up son and he lived in a two-bedroomed modern apartment near the Sportforum. They estimated his income as about fifteen thousand dollars a year in Ost-marks, and he would live very comfortably on that. There was no record of him being a party member, but he was a member of the journalists' union. They estimated his age as middle to late fifties.

A senior CIA operator had gone across and they had talked for ten minutes at the Friedrichstrasse S-Bahn station. Müller had been unwilling to give any indication of what he had to sell until finally the CIA agent had indicated that there would be no further meetings without some clue as to what was on offer. At that point Müller had told him to say one word to his seniors. He had whispered the word, and made the agent say it again and again until he said it correctly. The word had had no significance for the agent, nor for his seniors, but it was passed back to Langley, Virginia, in a brief routine report. The word was 'Chelyabinsk'.

The New York station chief flew to Berlin two days later and the negotiations began.

By the end of the second week they had hammered out a deal. A complete new identity, American citizenship, residence in California, a home costing no more than 40,000 dollars so far as agency responsibility was concerned, up-to-date social security documentation, payment at the rate of 25,000 dollars a year until he obtained employment, reducing at that point to a permanent pension of 15,000 dollars a year. At the beginning of the third week he had added two further demands. The first of these was that he should be accompanied by his eighteen year old girl-friend. he gave one more piece of information to back-up his demands. A date. December 1957.

When the additional information was passed to CIA HQ at Langley they had responded immediately with instructions to meet all Müller's demands without argument. His second condition they said they would deal with themselves.

Boyle was surprised when he arrived at his club to be shown upstairs to one of the private rooms. As he shook Parker's hand he said, 'I didn't realize, of course, that you were a member.'

'I'm not, my boy. Some friends arranged it for me.'

Boyle was just vain enough to appreciate, at his age, being called 'my boy' by a man who he suspected was not more than ten years his senior.

'Let me order some drinks.'

Parker shook his head, smiling. 'It's my invitation. The drinks are ordered. And so is the meal. I gather that "truite d'amande" would not come amiss.'

Boyle smiled. 'I think somebody must have been tittle-tattling.'

Parker laughed 'Let's say a few discreet inquiries. Ah, here's the drinks.'

43

When the waiter had laid out the food and served them, Parker said, without looking up from his plate:

'I was *asked* to make contact with you, James.'

'Oh. Asked by whom?'

'Some people in Whitehall who need your help.'

'Good grief, it's many a long year since my chambers got a brief from the Treasury Solicitor's office.'

'It's not legal help they need.'

'Then I'm afraid they've got the wrong man, my friend. I have no expertise beyond the law and some might query even that.'

'People trust you, James. All sorts of people.'

Boyle dabbed his lips, folded his napkin and laid it aside.

'You'd better tell me what it's all about.'

'Let's make ourselves comfortable in the armchairs.'

As Boyle stood up he said 'I never like discussions that need armchairs, you know. There's nothing that can't be better discussed across a table. However . . .'

When they were both sitting, Parker offered Boyle a cigar, and when he declined, lit one for himself. It was one of those ritual lightings, Boyle noticed, the kind that the more sophisticated criminals perform before they indulge in the impertinence of telling you what they want you to say in court. A rolling of cigars to the ears, a sniff for fragrance, and then the clipping ceremony, or the piercing ritual, and finally the match and the blue haze. A device, Boyle thought, to allow third-rate minds to collect their thoughts. Eventually it was over and Parker leaned back and looked at him.

'Would you spare some old friends two or three days of your time, James?'

'Which old friends, and why?'

'D'you remember a German named Otto Lemke?'

'Of course. I lived with him for nearly four years.'

'Did he keep in touch with you?'

'A few Christmas cards, but that was a long time back.'

'I don't know if you remember, but we gave him a new identity and a job as a German civilian with a Military Government detachment.'

44

'I do remember.'

'Well, he became a journalist a few years later. On the Hanover Kurier. A sports journalist. He was sent to cover some event in East Berlin and he met a girl, and a few months later he crossed over. He married her and they had one child. A son. They live in East Berlin. He's quite a well-known sports journalist now. To cut a long story short he wants to come back to the West. He's offered some information if we'll bring him over and support him.'

When Parker stopped Boyle had pursed his lips. 'That shouldn't be difficult.'

'I agree. It *shouldn't* be, but unfortunately, our old friend Lemke has laid down some conditions and one of them is the reason I'm here . . . apart from the pleasure of seeing you again, of course.'

Boyle sat quite still, waiting for Parker to continue, his grey eyes showing minimal curiosity. Parker knocked off a long cylinder of ash in the ash-tray. Then he looked up at Boyle.

'One of the conditions is that he won't come over unless you are in charge of the operation.'

'Me. For God's sake. Why me?'

'He trusts you.'

'And who in hell is *he* to lay down conditions?'

'I'm afraid that the information he's got is important enough for us to agree to almost anything he asks for. And over the last ten days he's begun to get cold feet, so it's urgent, as far as we are concerned, that we get him out.'

'Am I allowed to ask what his information is about?'

'We can put you fully into the picture if you could find it possible to help us. Otherwise it's better that you don't know.'

'I can guess, Parker. Like all these wretched people he'll be betraying the people who give him a living.'

'I'm afraid it's more than that. Much more.'

Boyle shrugged his shoulders in the chair as if he were uncomfortable.

'How do you come into it?'

45

'I give advice from time to time, and they knew that you and I had worked together during the war. They wanted the approach to be as informal as possible.'

'Why should it need to be informal?'

'So that if you refused, your refusal would not go down on the record.'

Boyle rubbed one hand along the back of the other. He wanted to say that he was indifferent to what went on the record. Whatever 'the record' might be. But Parker was no fool. Declining would have to have some sensible, rational basis.

'Unfortunately it would not be possible to give my time at the moment. There are decisions I have to make that cannot be postponed.'

Parker's hand hovered over the ash-tray, the long ash from his cigar just touching the lip, it fractured and fell in one piece, and he ground it slowly to powder before he looked up at Boyle again.

'You mean the offer of a judgeship?'

'How on earth did you know about that?'

Parker sighed. 'I feel I'm handling this very badly, James. I've been pussy-footing around when I ought to have been direct. So . . . let me say first of all that this operation has the highest priority on both sides of the Atlantic. To say that it is at cabinet level with both countries is only an indication of how much we want this information. But Lemke won't budge without you. He wants out desperately, but he's scared. Like I said, you're the only one he trusts. If it were anyone but you we could offer them whatever they wanted – money, titles – anything. The powers that be asked me what would tempt you. There was only one thing that I could think of.'

Boyle's grey eyes looked at him unblinking. 'And what is that?'

'To persuade you that doing this is a matter of duty. And to tell you quite openly that we are at your mercy. There is no pressure that we could, or would, apply; and no reward that we can offer that you would find significant. Not that rewards will not be offered I can assure you.' Parker shrugged and let his hands fall to his knees. 'And there I rest my case.'

Boyle opened his mouth to admonish the cliché then thought better of it. 'How long would it take, Parker?'

'A week. Ten days at the most.'

'Let's say that in principle I will give you ten days. I should charge normal brief fees for that time of course.'

'Would you meet my masters tomorrow after court?'

'Yes. Where?'

'Eighteen Ebury Street. Just knock. We'll be waiting for you from four-thirty onwards.'

CHAPTER SIX

The girl was very pretty. About 17, and typically German. Blue-eyed, straw-blonde hair and full-breasted. By no means a Brunhilde, more a Penthouse Pet.

Apart from the picture of Elvis Presley the small room was typically German too. Chintzy and clean, and there were frills round the base of the small dressing-table in front of which the girl stood. Both her arms were raised as she fiddled an elastic band on to the final knot of her pigtails. The mirror was a small triptych, but the image it gave back was more carnal than spiritual. She wore a lacy white half-cup bra that seemed to offer her magnificent breasts like exotic food on a dish. A thin white suspender-belt supported a pair of tan nylon stockings. The get-up might have been considered faintly old-fashioned in Chelsea, but she wasn't in Chelsea, and every man she'd ever been with had said that it really did something for her. And it had done quite a lot for the men too.

The young man stood behind her, watching the reflection of her body in the mirrors, and as she took the last elastic band from between her even white teeth he had slid his hand between her legs. For a few moments she had arranged her pig-tails and for a few more she had just stood patiently with a half-amused smile on her face. Then she said amiably, 'For God's sake, Karl, enough's enough.'

'You wanted it last night, Ushi.'

'Of course I did. I want it now, but there isn't time. I've got to be at that bloody office by nine.'

'You just can't wait to have it with that old man, can you?'

She turned angrily. 'He keeps me, which is more than you'll ever do. You get it for free.'

Then, seeing his sullen look, she shrugged and smiled. 'D'you really want to do it again?'

He nodded, and she went over to the unmade bed.

She lay back and opened her long legs. When he had finished he lay alongside her and reached over for his cigarettes and lighter and lit a cigarette for each of them.

'Can you get me a ticket for the Dortmund match on Thursday?'

'I expect so, but he's edgy at the moment.'

'What about?'

'I don't know. Probably his wife playing him up.'

'Why don't you find a job somewhere else?'

She laughed softly. 'You're jealous, aren't you?'

'Maybe. You've been my girl for two years until he came along.'

She sat up. 'For Christ's sake don't try that crap, Karl. For two years you've been screwing me, but I haven't been the only one. Neither have you. Müller is for real. He's got money, and influence, and if you try to mess that up you won't know what's hit you, boy. I'll see to that.'

He pulled her on top of him and kissed her. 'I won't mess it up, Ushi.' And she spread her legs and let him take her again.

Müller closed the office at six and took her to the Café Warschau to meet a Pravda man who was doing a feature on the East German swimming team for the Olympics. The two men chatted, comparing notes for half an hour, and their conclusion was that it would be the Romanians who would sweep the board in Moscow for both swimming and gymnastics. The Pravda man gave Müller captioned photographs of the Soviet swimming team.

Müller and the girl left the café at 7.15 and walked to Die Distel, and the pungent satirical jibes at the government, and the less pointed thrusts at Moscow had seemed to fit Müller's mood. The girl didn't understand half of them, but she laughed when he laughed.

They walked back arm-in-arm to Karl-Marx-Allee and walked up to the second floor where his offices occupied four rooms. The larger room at the back was where he

49

stayed most nights. He visited his home only at week-ends, and not always then.

He poured them vodkas and switched on the radio, and turned the dial until there was music. He stood listening. It was a girl with a bedroom voice singing 'Sag beim Abschied'; and when it was over he turned down the volume so that the music was almost inaudible.

He sat down on the comfortable leather couch, sighing.

'What's the matter, Otto? Are you bored, or tired?'

'I guess I'm bored, Ushi.'

'With me?'

He shook his head, smiling. 'I won't ever get bored with you, sweetie.'

'Are you going home at the week-end?'

'No. I'm going to Dresden to cover the football. D'you want to come?'

'If you want me to.'

'I'll buy you those boots that you wanted.'

She put down her glass, and without looking at him she said, 'Will you ever leave her, Otto?'

He leaned back and looked at the girl.

'And if I did, what then?'

She shrugged. 'That would be up to you.'

'Would you marry me?'

'Of course. I've said many times that I would.'

'Sure. You said yes when it wasn't possible. But what if it *is* possible?'

'Then it is still yes.'

'You mean that?'

'Of course. Why do you doubt it?'

'Because I'm older than your father. That's why.'

'Why should that matter. It's you I want.'

'What about all those boy-friends you had when I met you? Young Karl and the others.'

'To hell with thèm. They're kids not men. There would never be security with them.'

'I've had offers that would pay well, where nobody would know us.'

50

'What sort of offers?'

'Sports columnist. My usual stuff.'

'Where?'

'All sorts of places – *Corriere della Sera* are interested. I've had interest from the Americans and from the Brazilians.'

'When are they talking about? Is it just talk?'

'In a month or six weeks if we wanted.'

'Would they give us permission?'

'Would who give us permission? And for what?'

'To leave. Don't we have to have permits?'

'All that would be fixed.'

'Including me?'

'Of course. I wouldn't consider it without you.'

She stood up and walked over to sit beside him, her face turned up to his, her hand on his thigh. And she said softly, 'Let's do that, sweetheart. A new life, just you and me.' And she closed her eyes so that she could think about what he had said as his hands fondled her breasts.

She went back alone to her small room on the Sunday evening after she and Müller got back from Dresden. She was admiring her long legs in soft brown leather boots when there was a knock on the door. She slid on a bath-robe to answer the door. It was Karl. She let him in and locked the door behind him. He looked angry and sullen.

'Where've you been? I've been looking for you for three days.'

'We've been to Dresden. I've only just got back.'

'We? Who's we? That old ram Müller I suppose.'

'You'll be an old ram one day, little boy. Anyway, why were you looking for me. The usual reason I suppose.'

'No, it wasn't. Well, not quite. You remember that actor we met at the Café Budapest? He fancies you. Wants to make a date. He'll pay in dollars.'

'How much?'

'Ten US dollars, honey.'

51

'You must be crazy, *mensch*. I wouldn't screw with Lenin for ten dollars.'

'Lenin's dead, sweetie.'

'So's your bloody actor as far as I'm concerned.'

'Do it as a favour to me, honey. He says he might be able to find me a job.'

'Jesus, what kind of *scheiss* are you, that I open my legs on the cheap for your bloody friends?'

'I thought you'd be pleased. You've often done it for less.'

'Go get stuffed, and the same to lover-boy.'

The tall young man stood there fumbling in his pocket.

'I got this for you, Ushi.'

He held out a gold ring, a man's signet ring, but as she took it she felt its weight. It was real gold, and heavy. It had the initials AH engraved on its boss.

She looked up at his handsome boyish face as he waited for her reaction. She knew how he would have earned it. It would be one of those rich western queers who hung around the cafés on Schönhauser Allee near the S-Bahn station.

She said softly, 'D'you want to stay the night?'

His face lit up. 'Thanks, Ushi. Thanks.'

She stood up and slid off the robe as she handed him the ring. 'You keep it. It's lovely. It'll suit you better, honey.'

It was 2 a.m. before he had had enough, and she watched him as he stood, naked, making them both a cup of coffee. She realized that she would miss him. It wasn't a real relationship, just sex. But his body was beautiful, like the Greek statue she had seen in the Bode museum. And unlike her relationship with Müller, Karl was dependent on her. Sometimes in the past two years they hadn't seen one another for two or three weeks, but it was an easy-going relationship and they would take up again as naturally as if there had been no break. And the men he had brought to have sex with her had been good-class men and no trouble. Maybe she could squeeze some money out of Müller for him before they left. She realized that Karl was going to be really upset when she was no longer around. He was two years older than she was in years, but he was childlike in reality. The first time he had gone to bed with her she had been faintly surprised that he knew what to do. But he had done it with practised skill and she knew that she would miss that too.

When they were drinking their coffee she said, 'You mustn't depend on me, Karl. Have you got other girls?'

'I find business sometimes for girls at the Café Budapest but I don't sleep with them.'

'What about that pretty one with black hair. Heidi, Helena or whatever she calls herself these days.'

He was blushing and she smiled. 'Come on. No need to be shy.'

'Just once or twice. She asks *me*, not me ask her.'

'D'you earn enough to live on now?'

'Almost enough. Why do you ask all these questions?'

'I may be away for a few months.'

'For the Moscow Olympics in the summer?'

'Maybe longer than that.'

'But you'll be coming back.'

'Of course.'

But she had hesitated just a fraction too long, and the young man saw it. 'This is that bastard Müller, isn't it?'

'Maybe.'

'It is. It *could* only be him.'

She reached up to stroke his cheek, 'Think of *me*, Karl, it's a chance for security for me. Something solid. A real home. Don't cry, my love. It may not happen.'

'Why should you go away, Ushi? You could be with him here.'

'He's got a wife and son.'

'I know, but he can get a divorce or something.'

'That takes time.'

His head came up. 'That means there isn't time. You'll be going soon.'

She kissed him gently and lifted his hand to one of her breasts and murmured, 'Love me again, Karl. Love me a long time.'

CHAPTER SEVEN

You were privileged and important if your office was on the top floor of the long, curved, glass-fronted KGB headquarters building off the Moscow Ring Road, and the equipment and furnishing was typical of any big United States corporation.

Yuri Galitsyn's office was one of the smallest on the top floor. There was a two-metre teak desk-unit, three telephones, and two long teak tables with neat piles of files in plastic covers. Most of the covers were a pale pink, but others were blue, green, or translucent. The file cover on his desk was black, and he leafed over the few pages of a typed report, referring back from time to time to the first page.

He reached for the black internal phone and dialled four numbers.

'Galitsyn here. This report from Berlin that you passed to me. Half the necessary information is missing.'

'Such as what, comrade?'

'The youth Karl Unger, is he a party member? There is no suggestion of why Müller might be defecting.'

'There isn't anything more.'

'Is there any surveillance on Müller?'

'There has been, but only for two days.'

'And?'

'And nothing, I'm afraid.'

'I'll initial it and send it back to you. But notify me if there are any indications from the surveillance.'

'OK.'

Galitsyn hung up, frowning at the Americanism.

It was less than two hours later when Mazurov knocked and came in, a half-sheet of paper flapping in his hand.

'Your magic touch again, Galitsyn.'

He put down the paper so that it faced Galitsyn who leaned forward to read it.

It was a typewritten record from the KGB office in East Berlin. Müller had gone to a newspaper shop in Heinersdorf. Had been there for an hour in one of the upstairs rooms. There were no girls on the premises, but a suspect CIA cut-out had left the shop an hour after Müller had left. It was assumed that the CIA contact had not been logged-in because it was a single-man surveillance who had to eat and relieve himself from time to time. The shop was suspect but had a low interest grading.

Galitsyn leaned back. 'What information can a sportswriter have that would interest the CIA?'

Mazurov grinned. 'Probably trying to check on the sex of the Soviet women discus-throwers.'

Galitsyn didn't smile. He didn't like jokes about sex, or about women. He looked up.

'Leave this with me. I'm going to Berlin on Thursday. I'll see what's going on.'

Galitsyn looked out of the plane's window as it banked to come into Schönefeld. Berlin stretched under the wing like a model railway layout. He hated the trips he had to make to Germany. He hated the Germans. The East Germans as much as the West Germans. And he particularly hated Berlin and Berliners, whichever side of the wall they came from. He didn't hate consciously, but as naturally as he breathed. When he was still in the army and an army psychiatrist was checking him after the KGB had applied for his transfer, the oaf had gone through the 'do you love your mother better than your father' bit and finally got around to hates. And Galitsyn had said he had no hates. Just Germans. The psychiatrist had smiled. 'Not all Germans surely?'

'Yes. All Germans.'

'Because they killed your parents?'

'Yes.'

'What about Germans who were not even born then?'

'The same. Makes no difference.'

'What about the Germans who were killed in Dachau and Sachsenhausen?'

'The same.'

The psychiatrist had hesitated for a moment as if he might put another question, then he had scribbled for several minutes at the foot of his report. Galitsyn's commanding officer had covered up the report except for the last lines of the scribbled note. What he had shown to Galitsyn said: 'This officer's parents were killed by the Germans in the Great Patriotic War, and it appears to have left him with a psycho-neurotic aversion to all Germans. No clinical features. No evidence of "derived emotion". Not auto-nomic. This psychosis should be borne in mind if this officer is required to deal extensively with German personnel.'

The plane was the first of the big Ilyushins that the Polish airline had been allocated, and there were photographers at the airport. He waited in his seat until the photography was over and then walked with the steward to the black Zil that was waiting for him at the service hangar.

He had been driven to the old-fashioned house near the Jungerfernbrücke. It had been rebuilt in 1950 exactly as it had originally stood before Berlin lay in ruins. It stood in its own grounds, but it was taken for granted that despite the security most Germans in the area knew that it was a KGB house.

Galitsyn wasted no time and read carefully through the latest reports. He walked into the outer office and told them to arrange for him to see Karl Unger at the small rendezvous house they kept in nearby Stalaustrasse.

Galitsyn sat across the table from the young German, slightly surprised at his boyish, open face, and his diffident manner. Informers generally came either greasy or tough. He made the effort and used the youth's christian name.

'Let me say first of all, that you were quite correct, Karl, to report this matter to the police. It may be important, or quite innocent, but you have done your duty.'

'Thank you, comrade colonel.'

56

'How did you know that I am a colonel?'

'Your man said so.'

'Did he give you my name?'

'No, comrade.'

'D'you smoke, Karl?' And he proffered a pack of 'Lucky Strikes', but the youth shook his head.

'Tell me about the girl, Karl.'

'Like I told the police, she was my girl until Müller came along. She sees me sometimes, and she hinted that they were going away. Both of them.'

'Did she say where?'

'She said it like it was overseas but she didn't say any particular place.'

Galitsyn recalled the police report on Unger that said he pimped for several prostitutes.

'How does the girl earn her living?'

'She's Müller's secretary.'

'Any other sources of income?'

'No.'

The youth's blue eyes had the extra frankness of the habitual liar but Galitsyn left the subject without more questions.

'Does she have a sexual relationship with Müller?'

'Yes.'

'How do you know?'

'She told me, and anyhow . . .'

'Go on.'

'I just know,' he said lamely, and Galitsyn made a note on the pad that Unger had probably introduced the girl to Müller. He looked up at the German.

'Did you know Müller before he took up with the girl?'

'Yeah. I knew him for a couple of years before.'

'How was that?'

'I got a trial for Berlin juniors and he wrote a piece about me.'

'This was football?'

'Yes.'

'What happened to all that?'

Unger shrugged. 'They didn't take me on.'

'D'you like Herr Müller?'

'Not particularly.'

'Do you *dislike* him?'

'Not enough to tell lies about him, if that's what you mean.'

'How much, then?'

'How much what?'

'How much *do* you dislike him?'

Unger sat silent.

'Are you jealous or angry about him and the girl?'

'A bit.'

'Have you told her that you have reported this to the police?'

'Jesus, no. She'd kill me.'

'You *mean* kill you, or just that she'd be angry?'

'She'd do something. I know that.'

'Does the girl live with Müller?'

'She stays with him a lot of the time. They sleep at his offices. But she's got a room of her own.'

'Where is it?'

'Just off Karl-Marx-Allee in Markenstrasse. Number forty-seven, room seven.'

'Is it a nice room.'

'Yeah – not bad.'

'Well, Karl, I want you to tell her you'd like to take over the room when she leaves.'

'I couldn't afford it.'

'You don't have to, we will pay the rent for a couple of years until you get established.'

'That would be great. D'you want me to keep an eye on Müller?'

'No, that won't be necessary, we'll do that. Just let us know if you hear anything about him leaving. Selling furniture or anything like that.'

After the boy had gone Galitsyn sat studying the photographs of Müller. Accepting a Writers Union award at a dinner.

Chatting to Olga Korbut by parallel bars. Holding up a stopwatch to the camera with his arm around the shoulders of a grinning athlete. And a couple of recent photographs taken as he came out of his office, and walking with the girl down Karl-Marx-Allee. There was a not too clear record shot of him leaving the newspaper shop in Heinersdorf.

Galitsyn shoved them all back in the file cover. Müller would go under light surveillance now, but there were more things to deal with in Berlin than sportswriters, defecting or otherwise.

CHAPTER EIGHT

Boyle hated the waste of time of social chit-chat that people seemed to feel necessary before they got down to business. But it wasn't long before Parker pointed to the round table, and there was a scraping of chairs as they sat down.

Parker sat opposite Boyle, and on his left was Martin Hamilton who was acting-liaison with MI6: and Bill Autenowski, liaison from the CIA's London bureau. Parker looked very much at ease with the two men and Boyle wondered how 'retired' he really was. Then Parker started.

'As you know, gentlemen, I have asked Mr Boyle to help us with our problem concerning Müller, the man who Boyle and I remember as Otto Lemke.

'Boyle has agreed to give us some of his time. A period of ten days was mentioned. I have told him the importance we attach to Müller's information, and the conditions Müller has laid down if he is to co-operate. But I have given him no information regarding the subject matter. Do I have your agreement to do that, gentlemen?' He looked first at the American.

'I'd like to ask Mr Boyle a couple of questions first, Mr Chairman.'

'Go ahead.'

The American looked at Boyle. 'Are there any restrictions on you travelling overseas apart from questions of personal convenience.'

'Not so far as I know.'

'Does that include the Soviet Union?'

'It includes anywhere. Maybe Parker could confirm that.'

Parker nodded. 'There are no restrictions of any kind from security.'

The American went on, 'Would your availability cover the third week in May?'

'I should have to rearrange my cases to do that, but most of them are on behalf of government departments so I imagine there's no insuperable problem.'

The American nodded to Parker. 'It's OK by me, sir.'

Parker turned to look at Hamilton who shook his head. 'No problems with my people.'

Parker turned back to the American. 'Bill, you brief James now on the basics.'

Autenowski closed his eyes for a moment and then looked at Boyle. 'Does the word "Chelyabinsk" mean anything to you?'

'Sounds Russian or Polish, that's all.'

'Chelyabinsk is a town in the Soviet Union. It's in the South Urals, due south of Sverdlovsk. I don't suppose before 1958 that even specialists on Soviet affairs had ever heard of Chelyabinsk.

'In 1958 there were rumours of a nuclear disaster in Chelyabinsk. The rumours made brief paragraphs in the newspapers. They were hotly denied by the Soviet Union, and in the US important specialists dismissed them as CIA propaganda. In the UK the chairman of the United Kingdom Atomic Energy authority, Sir John Hill, referred to the rumours as "science-fiction" and a "figment of the imagination".

'The CIA evaluation was that it *had* happened and that hundreds of square miles of that area had been devastated. Towns and villages would have completely disappeared, and hundreds of people would have died at the time of the explosion, and thousands would have died since, from the effects of strontium-90 and caesium-137.

'When we asked Müller what information he proposed trading he gave us first, just one word – "Chelyabinsk". Later he gave us a date – December 1957. We assume that that was the date of the disaster. It fits the rumours and our own assessment.

'We want anything we can get on Chelyabinsk. Anything. And we want Müller out quickly.'

Boyle raised his eyebrows. 'It's not for me to comment on

61

any of this. It's out of my province. Tell me how I can help.'

Autenowski leaned forward, his arms on the table.

'He's absolutely adamant. Unless *you're* in charge of getting him across the border it's no dice. And that means him and the girl. We may have to bring them over separately of course.'

Boyle frowned. 'I'm a bit old for that kind of game.'

'You don't have to be involved in that. All he asks is that he meets you, talks with you, and that you are in charge of the operation to get him across. You don't need to be physically involved.'

'And provided he tells you what he knows he will be looked after? You will meet your promises to him?'

'Sure we will. It's a joint operation anyway. Your people are as involved as we are. It's just that he contacted CIA in Berlin and we've kept the contact because we have to eventually supply the things he wants.'

Hamilton said, 'He'll get what he's asked for, Mr Boyle. Provided he doesn't play games.'

'What sort of games?'

'Holding back information. Upping the prize money. There'll be quite a period when we're checking him out. He could be a KGB plant. He's a greedy man. They sometimes get a bit silly. The last one we had decided that he'd add a little extra to his shopping list. He'd seen *Bonnie and Clyde* in Stockholm. Wanted to sleep with Faye Dunaway.'

Boyle was not amused. 'What did you do?'

Hamilton smiled and nodded towards Autenowski. 'They found a young lady for us who looked remarkably like Miss Dunaway.'

Boyle said, 'Why did you ask me about the third week in May and Moscow?'

It was Hamilton who answered him. 'One of the TV companies has a team going to Moscow the third week in May to finalize both the technical and legal details of coverage of the Moscow Olympics. The main contracts have already been signed and these negotiations are to clear up the odds and ends. The Soviets always drag their feet so there will be plenty of time. Müller, as a sportswriter, has every reason to go to Moscow to make his final arrangements for covering the Olympics. They'll give him all the facilities he wants.

'We had in mind that you should go with the TV negotiating team as one of the legal advisers. We could brief you about our escape plan for Müller and you could pass it on to him.'

Boyle reached down and brought up a thin tan-coloured leather case. He snapped open the clasps and took out a leather-bound diary. He opened it, riffled through the pages, found what he wanted and slowly read the entries. Then he looked up.

'There are two cases that I couldn't reasonably pass to colleagues. On the twenty-first there's a judgement which may get appealed. The two Arabs. And on the twenty-fourth there's the start of a long case. A bit of a dog's breakfast under the 1934 Incitement to Disaffection Act, with Section Two, Clause One thrown in as a long stop. Fourteen accused.'

There was a long silence and then Parker turned to Hamilton. 'Can you get the Solicitor-General to take these over?'

Hamilton nodded. 'I'm sure we can fix that.'

Boyle gritted his teeth at the use of the word 'fix' used in any legal context. It could be overheard by the ignorant, and misconstrued.

Parker looked at Boyle. 'Could we say that we can plan forward on this basis?'

Boyle nodded, 'Yes.'

A bound copy of the overall TV contract with the Soviet Union was delivered by hand to Boyle's chambers the next morning, together with several sheets of queries to be raised by the negotiating team. He spent the week-end studying them carefully and phoned Parker at his home on the Sunday evening to arrange the next meeting.

A private room had been booked at the Travellers and after a quick meal they had settled round the coffee table.

Despite the silence as they waited for Boyle to speak he leafed slowly through his notes as if he were unaware of any pressure. Then he looked at each one of them before he spoke.

'There is a reference to "residuals" that I don't understand. What does it mean? The first mention is on page seventy-two, para four.'

Parker looked across at Autenowski who said, 'In this particular case it means the TV company's right to use material in other programmes in the future. Including programmes other than sports programmes.'

'There might be other jargon that I don't understand that could come up during the negotiations. What do I do about that?'

Parker nodded. 'It will be made clear on the TV team that you are attached to them as a non-specialist, mainly concerned with covering Foreign Office interests.'

'And where do I meet Lemke?'

'We'll cover that the day before you leave. We shall also give you a telephone number that you must refer to if you miss any contacts or you have any other problems. You will have a code to use with that contact and they will pass you instructions on meeting places and times. But they will not be able to give you guidance on negotiating with Lemke. We must leave that to your discretion.'

'What assistance can I expect from the embassy?'

'None, I'm afraid. Nothing beyond what we could do for any other business visitor.'

'Have we an up-to-date photograph of Lemke that I could study?'

'We have, but we shall arrange for you to see him without making contact before you meet him in Moscow.'

'Where will this be?'

'In Berlin. East Berlin.'

'I see.' Boyle looked back at his notes but Autenowski interrupted his reading.

'We shall give you details of the escape route for Lemke before you meet him in Moscow. You'll have to memorize them, and the code-word, but we'll brief you on that after Berlin.'

'How many days will Berlin take?'

'You'll be there and back in two days.'

'When?'

'Next week-end if that's agreeable to you.'

'And Moscow?'

'Two weeks from now – the third week in May.'

Hamilton, the MI6 liaison man, had leaned forward. 'We shall be keeping an eye on you in Moscow. But it will be a passive eye. We couldn't help you at all.'

'Do you expect that I might need help?'

'Not at all. Your contacts with Lemke will be brief and apparently accidental. We shall go over a street-plan of Moscow with you before you go, and we shall suggest suitable meeting places, but Lemke knows Moscow from previous visits. He'll be very, very cautious.'

Boyle looked across at Parker. 'And what am I supposed to discuss with Lemke?'

Parker nodded to Autenowski who sat with his big hands on his knees, his elbows splayed out, and he sat leaning forward as if he felt he might need to convince Boyle of something.

'The arrangements that we have made with Lemke are step by step procedures. He will accept that the operation starts when he sees you in Berlin. There'll be no contact – he'll see you, and that's it. After that he will send us token evidence of the material he is offering. When we have evaluated that we shall arrange the contact between you and him in Moscow.

'He has a period of five days to hand over the material to you, and arrangements will be made for you to pass on that material. If the first batch is satisfactory we shall ask you to confirm to him the details of what we are offering in return. Provided he accepts you will give him the code-word and details of his escape route. He will then hand over the rest of his material and return to East Berlin to await our signal.'

'How does he get that signal?'

65

'It will be a code-word and a piece of music on the Voice of America.'

'How do I contact my contact in Moscow?'

'We shall give you a telephone number and a code set. The contact will arrange rendezvous in conjunction with Lemke. You will pass on the material immediately. You'll get instructions on where to leave it.'

'Do the TV team know what I'm doing?'

'Absolutely not.'

'Does the embassy know?'

Autenowski looked across at Hamilton who hesitated for a moment and then said, 'I can't discuss that, sir.'

Boyle's cold eyes turned to Parker. 'I'd still like to know exactly what happens if anything goes wrong.'

'What had you got in mind, James?'

'Nothing. Anything. What happens if I am arrested or Lemke is arrested?'

'If Lemke were arrested the operation would be aborted immediately.'

'And if I were arrested?'

'If it were sufficiently advanced the operation would continue, and Lemke could come over.'

'And what about me?'

'The embassy would make the normal fuss.'

'No more than that?'

'I'm afraid not. If we made more than the normal protests it would only confirm their suspicions.'

When Boyle was silent Autenowski said, 'You won't do anything suspicious, Mr Boyle. You will have Lemke's material for less than an hour on any occasion and possibly you may not have it for more than five or ten minutes. It would be a million to one chance that they could do more than hold you on suspicion for a few days until the diplomatic wheels had turned.'

Boyle looked at Autenowski as he sometimes looked at defending counsel in court. A look of contempt that included eyes and mouth and one raised eyebrow.

'Mr Autenowski, I don't know what the ethical codes are

in your country, but in Great Britain the courts would not favour a judge or Queen's Counsel who had been stupid enough to get himself involved in espionage; or careless enough to be even falsely accused of some misdemeanour or crime by the Soviet police.'

Hamilton moved in hurriedly to divert the pressure from the CIA man, 'You're thinking of how the KGB framed Commander Courtney, sir?'

'I assure you I am not thinking of any such thing. I am thinking about *my* reputation.'

Parker leaned back in his chair to give some air of relaxation as he prepared to draw the lightning.

'Would you be happier, James, if we gave you a different identity? We could do that.'

'Why wasn't that suggested in the first place?'

'It didn't seem necessary, and it introduced a complication that would make things more vulnerable than they need be. When their embassy checks you for a visa in your own identity there will be no problems. If we create a false identity and covering documents we open a whole new area of danger. Especially as there is so little time for you to absorb a new identity.'

Boyle folded his arms across his chest. Parker noted the defensive gesture and realized that there were aspects of Boyle's character that they had perhaps overlooked. Despite his cold independence Boyle was so used to combating lies and attempts at deceit that he was vulnerable to the truth, disarmed by frankness when dissembling was possible.

'You're quite right, Parker. We'll leave things as they are.'

Boyle turned to look again at Autenowski. 'What form will Lemke's material be in?'

'Film. Minox film rolled tightly in a plastic tube about an eighth of an inch diameter and about half an inch long. About the size and weight of half a matchstick.' Autenowski smiled wryly, 'Easy to hide, and easy to lose.'

Parker stood up slowly as if it caused him effort. 'Let's have a whisky before we adjourn, gentlemen.'

As Boyle stood sipping the pale golden Glen Grant he was

conscious of a feeling that was almost euphoric. A feeling of suppressed excitement that fought with a sense of disloyalty to the mundane routine of his normal life that he had so carefully created. But he drank down the last half of his whisky in two impatient gulps. He never felt comfortable with groups of men, and could never find the small-talk that made such groups tolerable.

CHAPTER NINE

There were ten of them in the group: five of them were Turkish immigrant workers carrying bunches of flowers and boxes of chocolates for their girl-friends in East Berlin.

Boyle was last but one in the queue and he looked again at the four-language sign that warned travellers that they were 'now leaving the American sector'. The painted sign was chipped and tatty and some bright spark had scrawled the words 'and sex' after 'American sector'. The US military policeman wore a brassard on his arm that had the Stars and Stripes and the words 'Check-point Charlie' hand-embroidered in silk in a quaintly home-made style. He let them through two at a time.

When Boyle had shuffled forward to the 'Stop' sign an East German border guard waved him up to the barrier and as the pole was raised he stood looking at Boyle's passport. When he handed it back he gave Boyle a numbered slip and waved him on to the guardroom fifteen yards ahead. His passport and the slip had been fed into a chute behind the guard. While he was waiting he had to sign the customs declaration listing the currency that he carried on him.

A man in civilian clothes handed back Boyle's passport after comparing his face with the photograph in his passport. Boyle joined the next queue. One of the Turkish workers was led off, protesting, to an inner office. There was a poster of Lenin on the wall and an announcement that 7th July was the Day of the People's Police. Ten minutes later he passed through the customs control. There was another queue to check his currency declaration and then one more passport check before the last pole was lifted and he walked out into Friedrichstrasse.

He strolled slowly up towards Unter den Linden, and opposite the huge glass-fronted East German parliament building he stopped and looked at his watch. He was almost exactly on time. It was 14.55. A light breeze lifted his sparse hair as he stood there in the late spring sunshine. Lemke would be looking at him from some window or other until he moved on at 15.05. As he lifted his eyes to look at the sky he saw the blood-red reflection of the sun on the globe of the TV tower up toward Alexanderplatz. Exactly on the hour he crossed the broad street so that he was facing the huge white block of the Soviet Embassy. There were surprisingly few people in what had once been the heart of Berlin, and even fewer cars. Way down the far end of the Unter den Linden the black, red and yellow flag of the East German Republic fluttered from the top of the Brandenburg Gate. He counted off the seconds of each minute so that he need not keep checking his watch, and at the fifth minute past the hour he crossed the broad road and walked down the left-hand side of the Unter den Linden.

The leaves on the trees were that pale, clean, green of early May, and already one could barely see from one side of the broad avenue to the other. Half-way down he saw the sign. White plastic circles with the raised gold letters that spelt out CAFE. There was no name, just the single word set over a wide glass-fronted restaurant, its door standing open.

Boyle found a table in the street alongside the restaurant windows. He ordered a coffee, and the waiter also brought him a copy of the *Berliner Zeitung*. He sat facing the way he had come from the parliament building.

It was almost ten minutes later when he saw Lemke. He was walking with a girl. A very pretty girl who he felt must still be in her teens. Lemke looked surprisingly like he had looked all those years ago. His body was still slim, and his face almost unlined. He wore a pale brown shirt and brown hopsack trousers, and he carried a broad-checked sports coat over his arm. Lemke's brown eyes were looking at Boyle's face intently as he and the girl got nearer to his table; and as if sensing her companion's interest she too looked at Boyle as they passed. They walked past him again

70

ten minutes later, from the opposite direction, and this time, apart from a barely perceptible glance from Lemke, neither of them looked at him.

Boyle had followed his instructions precisely, eating a snack at the old Prinzessinen Palais and then walking to the State Opera. At no time was he away from the Unter den Linden.

The La Scala Opera and Chorus were giving their first performance in East Berlin of Verdi's Requiem, and only Boyle's hard currency had enabled him to buy a seat. The Opera House was packed, and Boyle noticed a sprinkling of uniformed US and British officers whose uniforms looked drab against the uniforms of the Russians and East Germans.

Neither the soaring music nor the Italians' passionate performance moved Boyle, and he sat uncomfortable and isolated in his seat when, at the end of the performance, the audience showered the stage with flowers and then rose to stand applauding for six or seven minutes. Boyle finally stood too, and clapped without enthusiasm, but there never had been music that could touch his heart. Words, either spoken or written, could stir him, but even with words it was their logic, their verity, that appealed, not their disposition.

He walked back in the darkness along Otto Gottwald-strasse, past the severed end of the Tiergarten and then turned left to Check Point Charlie. It took twenty minutes to pass back through the controls and the car had picked him up in Wilhelmstrasse. Ten minutes later he was at Temple-hof, and he was in London early the following morning.

Two days later Parker phoned him in the afternoon.

'Can we have a short meeting, James?'

'D'you want to come here to my chambers?'

'No. It wouldn't be secure.'

'Why not?'

'Our two friends might be under surveillance. There's no evidence of that, but we can't take risks.'

'Where do you want it then?'

'Can you be at the Commons in an hour?'
'Yes.'
'Ask for Room 117.'

A police sergeant escorted him to Room 117 and as the door closed behind him he saw that the others were already there.

It was an oak-panelled room with dim lighting and there was a framed photograph on the far wall. It was the Karsh portrait of Churchill.

Autenowski was fiddling with what looked like a TV screen and there were four chairs in line facing the apparatus. Hamilton was helping him, and Parker waved Boyle to one of the chairs. A couple of minutes later Autenowski pushed his hand through his floppy hair, and nodding to Boyle he sat beside him with a cable and a small control-switch in his hand.

'This is the first material from Lemke, and I thought you should see what form it takes. It's probably typical of what he'll be passing over to you.' He pressed the switch, and on the screen Boyle saw a small strip of negatives about half an inch by two inches.

'That's the film itself. Actual size. It's negative and we've not had time to make a positive.' Autenowski pressed the button again and there was an enlargement of the film strip, this time about six inches deep. Boyle could see the white lines between each frame and the outline of the sprocket holes. Then a single frame filled the whole screen. It was clearly a page of a document, and the type was white reversed on a black background. There was a title across the top in Cyrillic capitals. Autenowski said, 'That's the first page and the next item is a first translation.'

He pressed the button and the screen was bright with a page of typewritten text. There were more equations than text. Long equations, whose symbols even were beyond Boyle's comprehension. Across the top in capitals it read – 'Atomnaya Energiya May 1964 Vol 18, page 379. F. Rominsky'. Below the title it said. 'The calculation method for the distribution of radio-active contamination in water and bottom deposits of non-running water lakes'.

Autenowski snapped the button again and the screen went blank.

Boyle looked at Parker. 'Was this what you wanted?'

Parker nodded. 'Yes, our people are happy with this. If he has access to this then he could have what we want.'

'So what now?'

'Autenowski is going to explain the escape route and the code-words to you, and we should like the team to fly over on Sunday. You'll all fly to Amsterdam, and then take an Aeroflot flight to Moscow.'

'You'll need my passport for a visa.'

'We've done a new one for you, James. We've already got visas for everybody concerned.'

Parker and Hamilton pushed back their chairs and stood up. 'I'll see you again before you go, but phone me if there's anything I can help with.' Parker gave one of his brief smiles.

When the others had gone Autenowski stood up and looked at Boyle. 'Would you have any objection if we went over to my place, Mr Boyle?'

'Not at all.'

The taxi dropped them at the back entrance to the Park Lane Hilton and the lift took them up to the top floor. The American opened the double-locked door of his suite and as he switched on the light, holding the door for Boyle, he said, 'I get a lot of visitors and a hotel's good cover.'

As Boyle sat down all he could think of was the cost of the luxurious suite, and as Autenowski put the full whisky glass on the table in front of him he felt compelled to ask, 'How much does it cost, this place?'

Autenowski looked surprised. 'I don't recall exactly. I think we get special embassy rates. It's round a thousand bucks a week. Something like that.'

Boyle sat with the CIA man for almost two hours, poring over street maps, looking at photographs of streets and buildings that could be suitable meeting places and contact

73

points. He had been told a little about KGB surveillance methods and the normal checks of police and militia. Finally, he had been given an address in Magdeburg where Lemke was to go seven days after the codeword was broadcast on Voice of America.

CHAPTER TEN

Boyle met the TV negotiating team at Schiphol. Machin, who was leading the team, was in his middle thirties, red-haired and freckled, and wearing an olive-green corduroy suit that was so tight that it exaggerated his massive frame. Tudor Evans was younger, but his almost bald head and his gold-rimmed glasses gave him a vague donnish air that was re-inforced by his sober blue suit. Boyle looked up when they stopped in front of him.

'Mr Boyle?'

'Yes.'

'Right. I'm Terry Machin, and this is Tudor Evans.'

Boyle shook hands with them both and they sat down opposite him, their bags alongside them. Machin un-buttoned his bursting jacket to lean forward.

'I'm responsible for the overall network arrangements, and Tudor's with us to check the technical facilities. I gather you've been briefed on the main contract.'

'Yes. It doesn't seem to leave you much room for manoeuvre.'

Machin laughed. 'We've just had a couple of hours with the Dutch team. They got back from Moscow two days ago. They decided that if they made a strictly limited number of requests they would probably get what they wanted.' Machin looked at Boyle as if he expected him to hazard an opinion on how the Dutch had fared. When there was no response he grinned and said, 'They got nothing. Absolutely nothing. They said the Russians sat there po-faced and just said "Nyet" three times to their three requests. No discussion, no chit-chat. They didn't even get a courtesy visit to the sta-dium or the competitors' village.'

'How many points do we have?'

Machin laughed. 'We'd got twenty-one genuine points.

75

We've made it up to thirty-five. They're gonna find it tough to say "Nyet" thirty-five times. I just hope they say "da" to the ones we really want. We've sprinkled the extras throughout the list rather craftily, allowing the first three replies to be negative.'

'How much are the Dutch paying?'

'We don't know. Every country's keeping quiet in case they've got a specially good deal or a specially bad one. And the Russians aren't letting on either. Our estimate is that the Russians will be taking about a hundred million quid not counting gate-money, and odds and sods.'

'Are there any of our points that we *have* to get?'

Machin pursed his lips as he thought. 'I guess there's only one where we couldn't accept "no" for an answer, and that's the total separation between BBC facilities and ours. We negotiated separately and now we must stay that way.'

'Wouldn't you have been in a better bargaining position if you had negotiated jointly?'

Machin shrugged. 'Ours not to reason why, Mr Boyle. That's what our masters wanted.'

'Did the BBC pay more than your people?'

'I just don't know. I'd guess the other way round.'

Tudor Evans held up his hand. 'That's us.' The address system was announcing the departure of the Aeroflot flight to Moscow.

At Sheremetyevo they were met by a girl from Intourist, but despite the late hour the dour-faced customs officers had made them empty everything from their cases on to the metal bench. Every item was inspected, bottles of shaving lotion unscrewed and smelt, pockets checked, case-linings scrutinized and their files and papers slowly examined. Machin's copy of *Men Only* was looked at page by page and finally tossed on to a desk behind the bench. The customs officer turned and looked at Machin. 'Is to confiscate, yes.' And for the first of many times Boyle saw the red hair live up to its reputation as Machin said, 'Is ten roubles on black market, yes.'

For a moment the customs official looked as if he were going to call a man standing at the next desk. Then he waved his hand dismissively at the heap of clothes and oddments. 'You put back', and he walked away.

The Intourist driver took them to the Rossiya and the girl helped check them in. Machin protested against giving up his passport, but the girl calmed him down by explaining that it was not a whim, but Soviet law.

It was one o'clock when they settled into their adjoining rooms. Boyle was surprised at the sophistication of the hotel, and the modern decor of his bedroom. He was not the kind of man to have given much thought to the standard of life in Soviet Russia. Whatever it was, it was their business not his. But like most people he had a vague impression that it was an old-fashioned, grim city of dour-faced bureaucrats and an unsmiling public dedicated to digging up roads and manufacturing steel. He walked over to the window and pulled aside the curtains. In that moment he first sensed the power of the Soviet Union. Beyond the tops of the green-leaved trees were the Kremlin walls, and beyond them the floodlights picked out the domes and belfries of the Kremlin churches as if it were all some ornate setting for an opera. And Boyle realized that in one or more of those wedding-cake buildings the fate of a third of the world was decided every day. It looked so beautiful, but it was a cold and menacing beauty.

He slept uneasily until Machin knocked on his door at 7.30 the next morning.

They had been warned that their rooms would automatically be bugged. Not for any particular reason but just as a matter of routine and part of the hotel's permanent fixtures.

Machin sat on the bed while Boyle shaved and dressed.

'The Intourist girl says our meeting is at eleven so I'll go to our embassy and check if there are any messages for us. I gather it's not far if you fancy a walk.'

'No, I've got a bit of reading still to do.'

77

Machin stood up. 'See you in the foyer then. The girl will be there. Ten forty-five kick off.'

Boyle had a coffee in the café on the ground floor, and then he walked out of the hotel through the glass doors and out into the expanse of Red Square. He walked slowly towards St Basil's, skirting a group of sight-seeing soldiers, and a crowd of civilians who were being addressed by a guide, following his pointing finger towards the clock-tower to the left of the Lenin mausoleum. It was only 9.30 but already the square was busy with sightseers; a few obvious foreigners but the great majority Russians. They had warned him never to check if he were being followed, as even an apparent expectation or awareness of surveillance could alert the professionals of the KGB. At the history museum on the far side of the square he turned back.

He had seen the telephone kiosks as he walked across the square. Only one was being used. He dropped two copecks in the box and then dialled the number. It rang only once before a voice with a heavy accent answered in English and he said slowly and carefully, 'On the twelfth day of Christmas my true love gave to me . . .'

There was only a moment's hesitation and then the voice said slowly, 'Three French hens tonight at ten.' Then the telephone was hung up at the other end.

The car took them with the guide up broad tree-lined avenues, and at the end of Kalinin Avenue turned into Ulitsa Tchaikovsky then up a wide, sweeping ramp to the entrance of a skyscraper that would have been at home in New York. Red flags were streaming in the breeze, and when Boyle leaned back to look up the face of the building the white clouds moving beyond its top gave him a spasm of vertigo so that he had to close his eyes. When he opened them the girl smiled. 'It has thirty-one storeys. It's the headquarters of the Economic Co-operation Council, what you call COMECON.'

They were escorted up to an office suite on the twentieth floor. The main room was about fifty feet long, and down its centre was a long teak table with modern chairs. About thirty on each side.

Three Russians were waiting there, and the Intourist girl introduced them as Andrei Saratov, chief negotiator; Nicolai Petrov, technical adviser; and Feodor Spassky, a sports producer from Moscow TV. The handshakes were entirely formal, and Saratov waved them into three seats at the rear end of the table, and the Russians sat down opposite them.

Saratov lit a cigarette, squeezing its long white cardboard tip and speaking without looking up. 'I am instructed to welcome you on behalf of the Olympic Co-ordinating Committee.' He said it as if he wished that he could dissociate himself from the greetings. He looked up at Machin. 'There is something you wish to confirm?'

'We have a number of points that we should like to discuss.'

'The American network is responsible for all hardware for themselves and European countries.' He smiled a smile that left his eyes cold and arrogant. 'They will not welcome requests for modifications at this stage.'

'I assume that the Soviet authorities can influence the Americans?'

'That would not be . . .' He searched for a word and then turned impatiently to the girl. ' . . . *v poryadke* what is *v poryadke*?'

The girl said, 'In order, correctly organized.'

Saratov nodded. 'It would not be in order for us to try to influence the Americans.'

Machin raised his eyebrows. 'Your ambassador in London told us that it was the Soviet government's intention to co-operate in every possible way.'

'Of course. Of course. Every co-operation.' Saratov smiled icily, his hands spread in appeal to sweet reason.

He looked at the girl as if he were signalling some message. 'What has the Ministry planned for this afternoon comrade Panova?'

'I think it was a visit to the main stadium, comrade Saratov.'

Saratov pursed his lips reflectively and then stood up looking at the girl. 'You take them to the complex and we meet again tomorrow morning. Say at eleven again. Where are they staying?'

'At the Rossiya.'

'We will meet there. Book us a room.'

Saratov nodded to the three visitors and left them without a good-bye or a handshake, and the other two Russians followed him in silence.

Machin's face was flushed with anger. 'So much for Russian charm.'

Boyle said quickly, 'He's probably only doing what he has been told to do.'

The Intourist girl led them to the lift, her face completely impassive.

By the time the report from Berlin was on Galitsyn's desk Lemke had already landed at Sheremetyevo from the Warsaw plane, but Galitsyn had had him traced. He was booked in at the Moskva but had been picked up at the airport by a sportswriter from Tass. They were now in the bar at the Rossiya.

Galitsyn walked from his temporary office in Dzherdzhinski Square down to Kuibyshev Street, and then into Red Square. There was still a long queue of people waiting to go in the Lenin mausoleum, and he walked slowly across the Square to where the glass front of the Rossiya caught the reflection of the setting sun.

He stopped in the foyer and then saw his surveillance man walk out of one of the lifts. He leaned against the counter as the man walked towards him.

'Müller's in the bar. Right at the far end. Kowalski left him about ten minutes ago. He's standing next to an Englishman. The Englishman's name is Boyle. He's booked into room eleven seventeen. I've put a girl up there on his floor, on the drinks table. Reception say Boyle is with a TV team that's here to make arrangements for covering the games. I haven't been able to check with immigration or the Sports Ministry.'

'I'll go up.'

Galitsyn had sent his man down to the KGB office in the basement to start the checks on Boyle. He sat with a vodka, sipping it slowly as he watched Boyle and the German. Their backs were turned to him and he couldn't see if they were talking together. He stood up and pushed his way through the tables so that he stood a few feet behind the two men. He could see their faces in the long mirror. They were not talking. Both of them were staring straight ahead. But all his training and all his instincts told him that in some way they were conspirators. Even their apparent unawareness of each other was an indication. But maybe the German couldn't speak English. He spoke Russian quite well, Galitsyn had that on the file.

Then Boyle put his head back to empty his glass, and putting it back on the counter he moved away from the bar, his hands in his jacket pockets, his shoulders slightly hunched as he walked out of the door. He pressed the lift button and waited. He entered the lift with a group of six tourists talking Swedish.

Galitsyn had gone down to the basement, called his office and asked for a surveillance team to be put on Boyle and the German.

The American leaning on the bar counter at the Rossiya had stepped aside so that Boyle could leave. He had asked the bartender for a Bloody Mary, and had made no attempt to hide his amusement when the bartender nonchalantly put the drink in front of him. He had held the glass in his left hand as the fingers of his right hand pulled away the adhesive tape and the tiny grey plastic cylinder from the underside of the bar-counter. The bartender had refused his tip when he left a few minutes later. The film was in the United States embassy's diplomatic bag for Berlin three hours later.

CHAPTER ELEVEN

Although the room was large, there was only the long table and its ten chairs, a modern sideboard and a low table with two telephones. The panelling on the walls looked like maple, and the carpet and window curtains were in a chocolate brown. There was no sound from the street ten storeys below.

The girl was wearing a white woollen sweater and a plaid skirt that Boyle felt was suspiciously like the Hunting Stuart. She sat alone by the window as they settled themselves around the table. There were handwritten place names that put the Russians on one side and the TV team on the other. Andrei Saratov sat opposite Terry Machin at the centre of the table. Nicolai Petrov was opposite Boyle and Feodor Spassky faced Tudor Evans.

Machin's pile of papers and files sat in solitary state in front of him. The Russians had neither notepads nor papers. Boyle wondered if the others had got the message. They didn't need papers or pads because they were not negotiating. The answers would all be negatives.

Machin took copies of a single sheet and handed them around as he spoke.

'It's not an agenda. Just a list of points that we should like to raise with you.'

There were a few minutes of silence while the Russians read down the lists carefully and slowly. It was Saratov who raised his head first.

'Most of these points you must take up with the Americans. As I explained yesterday, they are supplying all hardware to be used by foreign TV teams.'

Machin smiled back amiably. 'Of course; all we are asking is if you know what equipment has been chosen.'

Saratov shrugged and his indifference showed in his eyes. 'Is best you take up with the Americans.'

'Who is controlling the Eurovision satellite lines?' Tudor Evans looked across at Petrov who left the answering to Saratov.

'We shall control timing, period and programming, but the link will be operated by the Eurovision team. It's their arses you kick for quality, and it is with them you negotiate take-off.'

'Will there be simultaneous transmissions?'

'You mean alternative programming?'

'Yes.'

'That will be available by negotiation but only with Russian commentary on both channels.'

'We can apply English commentary at our control studio here.'

'No. Is not possible to do that.'

'There would be no technical problem for us doing that.'

Saratov pursed his lips without smiling as he shook his head. 'Is a question of USSR requirements not technicalities.'

Tudor Evans plunged in. 'Will all transmissions be compatible PAL and SECAM?'

'Of course.'

Machin leaned forward, his arms on the table as if he were physically excluding Boyle and Evans from the discussion.

'Can we look over the central control area while we are in Moscow?'

'I will ask if that is permitted.'

'There will be telex and telephone available in our own control studio?'

'All British TV will share control studio facilities. Two telex, and you can specify telephones at one hundred dollars per week per instrument. Plus call charges of course.'

Machin was smiling a smile of disbelief. 'You are not suggesting that we share a control studio with the BBC?'

Saratov leaned back in his chair. 'That is the arrangement already agreed.'

'No way, Mr Saratov. We have our own contract with your Ministry. It was signed eight months ago.'

'Maybe, but all individual country contracts are signed under the general conditions laid down by the Ministry of Communications.'

Machin leaned forward looking down the table to Boyle. 'What say you, Mr Boyle?'

'What Mr Saratov says is correct. However, that document in its introduction covering United Kingdom rights, bases the subsequent clauses on a document entitled in English – "Moscow Olympic Games 1980, rules for TV applicable to United Kingdom". The document specifies that because the appropriate Soviet authorities stipulated that the BBC and the Independent Broadcasting Authority must negotiate separate contracts, not joint contracts, that provision will be made by the Soviet authorities for separate control studios and other negotiated facilities.'

There were a few moments of complete silence and then Saratov nodded. 'I'll have that checked.'

'No need to do that, Mr Saratov. We have copies of the Russian original that you can use to refresh your memory.' Boyle slid the photocopies across the table. Saratov ignored them.

Machin watched Saratov's face to see how he would take the first sign of dissent. When there was no response Machin said, 'I should like to discuss camera sites and video-editing facilities.'

Petrov took a deep breath. 'Video-editing facilities will be available in individual control studios. The hardware will be United States origin. So far as camera sites are concerned you will be shown the site plans for all events. There will be no problems, I assure you.'

Machin nodded and looked back at Saratov. 'I'd like to raise the question of facilities for a news team.'

Saratov frowned. 'I don't understand. What news team?'

'A team to cover news items of a non-sports nature.'

Saratov shook his head in slow incomprehension. 'I don't understand.'

'We shall want to interview medal-winners, competitors in general on how they find their facilities. We shall want the views of spectators about various events. And interviews with visitors to Moscow.'

'There is no question of such a facility.'

'There is, Mr Saratov, you have already discussed it with the BBC team and with the United States team.'

'The BBC negotiations are between government and government. The United States have asked, and have been refused.'

'The BBC is not a government service, Mr Saratov.'

'As far as we are concerned it is.'

'It's a question of fact, Mr Saratov. The BBC is not a government broadcasting service. It is independent.'

'We cross swords over semantics, Mr Machin. I will speak to the Minister.'

'I should like an answer before we leave Moscow if that is possible.'

Saratov looked at Machin. 'You've had your answer, Mr Machin. It is no. Nevertheless I will make inquiries.'

'Can we talk about visas for our team?'

'That is for our embassy.'

'And freedom of movement for our team.'

'Will be the same as for all other foreign teams.'

'I understand that. I'm asking *what* freedom of movement we shall have.'

Saratov looked at Machin with arrogant antagonism as he spoke.

'You will have all the freedom of movement granted to tourists in the Soviet Union.'

'And the same photographic restrictions?'

Saratov sucked a tooth as he studied Machin's face. 'If you particularly want to film a missile site or military installations I am sure that your written application would be considered.'

Machin looked towards the window as if he were

considering carefully his reply. When he looked back at Saratov he said softly, 'We are here for the Olympic Games, Mr Saratov. However, I should like to think that we can show our viewers something of Moscow. The bridges across the river are a beautiful sight in the morning light, but they are also prohibited so far as photography is concerned. That is the sort of thing I had in mind.'

Saratov sighed, obviously untouched by the none-too-subtle flattery. 'Let me have specific cases and I will inquire.'

He stood up and looked at his watch. 'I'll take you back to your hotel, gentlemen. Perhaps we could meet again tomorrow morning.'

Autenowski, Hamilton and the two scientists sat waiting for the translation to be typed. Lucas was from the UK Atomic Energy Authority, and Klingman was in charge of the CIA's atomic intelligence unit.

Autenowski was on edge and felt a compulsion to talk, and he looked across at Klingman.

'Was the initial stuff of use, George?'

Klingman pushed his glasses back.

'Well let's say that it's very strong evidence. The data indicated that after a few months, strontium-90 was dominant. Rominsky was indicating that it was an experiment, but I'm sure that was bullshit. You don't contaminate two lakes of eleven and four square kilometres just to confirm some mathematical calculations.' Klingman shifted in his chair. 'And if you did, then by God you would be publishing papers about it regularly.'

The door from the outer office opened and a girl came in with four file covers. Autenowski stood up quickly and took them from her. He gave each of the three men a copy and sank back into his chair opening the buff cover of the file as he settled himself.

The first page was headed 'Voprosy Ichtiologii vol. 10, p. 1127; vol. 12, p. 174 by A. I. I'yento'. Autenowski saw that it dealt with plankton, water plants and fish in a contaminated lake. The heading on page four was 'Zoologicheskii Zhurnal vol. 49, p. 1370; Zhurnal Obshchei Biologii vol. 31, p. 698'.

Autenowski looked across at Klingman who was nodding as he turned the pages. It was nearly fifteen minutes before Klingman closed his copy of the file. He sat looking across at Lucas who was still reading. His glance went to Autenowski and he made an optimistic circle with his thumb and first finger. Five minutes afterwards Lucas had tossed his file at his feet and looked across at Klingman.

'That's it then, George.'

Klingman nodded. 'I guess so. I wonder how in hell he got this stuff.'

'Somebody must have advised him, a layman wouldn't see the significance.'

Autenowski grunted. 'How about you put Hamilton and me in the picture?'

Lucas waved a hand at Klingman. 'Go ahead.'

Klingman arranged himself comfortably. 'Well now. The first study is of the same lakes as the original one. But it's later. It measures the isotope concentration in the bones and muscles of more than a hundred pike. I won't go into why, but to get a hundred pike means a lake of between ten and twenty square kilometres. And to contaminate that size of lake to the levels he records of strontium-90, requires a contamination level of fifty million curies. You'd have to be crazy to try and handle that level of contamination for experimental purposes. The second paper underlines the other two. They were checking animals, and the list included the fact that they killed twenty-one deer from the contaminated area they were examining. To avoid depletion I'd guess that means at least one hundred deer were available. To support that number of deer takes at least one hundred square miles of terrain. The bang, gentlemen, was a big bang. D'you agree, Lucas?'

'Absolutely. And the lake is not running water so the contamination is in the basin. In the silt. And that means there were, or are, hundreds of millions of curies in the silt to contaminate the water to that degree. This explosion involved radioactivity equivalent to thousands of tons of radium. Nobody's going to let scientists put that load of junk around for experimentation.'

Autenowski leaned forward looking across at Klingman.

'How much more do we need, Professor?'

Klingman shrugged. 'We have a lot of questions to answer. We've definitely answered what *has* been the most important one – did it happen? I've no doubt now that it happened. But once that is established we get into some very deep water.'

Klingman pursed his lips and took off his glasses, cleaning the lenses with the ends of his tie. As he slid them back on he shrugged. 'Despite Hiroshima and Nagasaki nobody knows what present day nuclear explosions will do. We've got estimates, calculations, graphs and diagrams, and for once the experts don't disagree too violently. But the fact is they *are* estimates – nobody *knows*. And if you *know*, then by God you've got a massive advantage.'

Lucas took up the point. 'You can take it that the Soviets now have this information. And that doesn't just mean that they're a month or two, or even a year or two, ahead of the West. It means that they are permanently ahead of us. There are only three ways for the West to get this information. We wait for the first Soviet nuclear missile to hit the West. We suffer such an explosion ourselves. Or we get this information that Lemke is passing over to us. There ain't no other way.'

Klingman was knocking the dry ash from his pipe into the palm of his hand. As he emptied the ash carefully into a plant-pot he looked up at the others.

'Apart from that, we need to know what caused the explosion. Was it careless storage or . . .' His voice tapered off and he looked towards the window. Autenowski said quickly, 'Or what, Professor?'

Klingman shrugged. 'You know as well as I do what I almost said. Did the Soviets intentionally cause the explosion in non-laboratory conditions to get this vital information?'

'And kill and injure hundreds of their own people just to find out what happens? It isn't credible.'

Klingman shifted awkwardly in his chair to look at the CIA man.

'It may not be credible to you, Autenowski, but it's credible to me, and it will be credible to certain sections in your own HQ at Langley. And in the White House. And in the Pentagon. You're missing the point, my friend.'

'I'm sorry, sir.'

'Don't you realize the implications in this? If it was an accident maybe they not only know what happens after a nuclear explosion of this magnitude. They may also know what can cause an explosion in nuclear waste. Once they know *that* maybe they can *cause* such an explosion in our stocks of nuclear waste.' Klingman jabbed his finger towards Lucas. 'His people are building a massive expansion of their Windscale plant for treating the nuclear waste of half the world. The White House has exerted every pressure to dissuade them from doing this, but they have gone on with the programme regardless. This information from Chelyabinsk, whether it is an accident or not, might wake up the British public to the dangers they face. If the Soviets really *do* know how to cause such an explosion then you might as well start evacuating the north of England and the borders of Scotland right now. No wonder that our nuclear maniacs and theirs said that the original rumours about Chelyabinsk were hog-wash. Congress and the British Parliament would have been up in arms if they had known.

'Just think on this, Autenowski. If the Soviets know how to cause such an explosion then we can forget the SALT talks, détente, and all the rest of it. They've got us by the short and curlies as of now.'

Autenowski nodded. 'But if the Soviet people knew that they had deliberately triggered that explosion there would be an uprising.'

'Maybe, my boy, maybe. That's for you people and the politicians to work out. What matters is not was it deliberate, but do they know how to repeat it elsewhere. If it was deliberate then by God they can do it anywhere they choose. If it was an accident, have they found out how it happened? And if they *have*, then you can take it for granted that it can be duplicated. Up to now the only hazard about nuclear waste was leakage – contamination of the surrounding area. Nuclear waste is now in a new ball-game.'

Lucas nodded. 'Don't dismiss the possibility of a deliberate experiment, Autenowski. Stalin killed between one and two million Soviet citizens in his purges for far less reason.'

Autenowski stood up. 'I'll keep the operation going as long as I can. Maybe two more days will be enough. I daren't take longer with an inexperienced operator like Boyle.'

CHAPTER TWELVE

Boyle used the telephone in the kiosk again, and when the voice answered he said, 'On the eleventh day of Christmas my true love sent to me . . .'

There was a pause and then the voice said, 'Five gold rings at three today.'

And then the click as the speaker hung up.

Boyle stood in the kiosk, mentally going down the list of meeting places. Number five was the bench in Gorky Park that faced the ornamental island with the silver birches. The bench faced the little bridge. He remembered the photograph they had shown him where there was snow on the ground and the lake a steely blue.

He had eaten with Machin and Evans, and half-way through the meal the girl had come to their table.

'I come with the car for you in one hour and I am to ask if you like to see football match this evening. Moscow Dynamo are playing Spartak and you will be personal guests of Mr Saratov.'

Machin looked pleased. 'That would be great. Could we talk to some of the players?'

'I ask if it is possible.'

Boyle looked up at the girl. 'I'll take a rest this afternoon.'

The girl looked at him as if she was going to insist, and then smiled, 'But you come this evening, yes?'

'Of course.'

When the girl had gone Machin winked at Boyle. 'Maybe they're going to turn on the charm from now on.'

Boyle raised his eyebrows. 'More likely they're softening you up.'

Boyle watched them, when, an hour later, they walked out of the hotel with the girl. Back in his room he had checked the street map again.

*   *   *

Lemke was already there when Boyle turned into the right-angled bend in the path. He looked relaxed as he sat there smoking a thin cigar, watching two boys with a paper boat who played at the edge of the lake, under the watchful eye of an old 'babushka' dressed in black.

As Boyle sat down Lemke said, 'We talk for no longer than two minutes. Are your people satisfied?'

'I've no idea, Otto. I assume they are.'

'Did they tell you what it's all about?'

'Only in general terms.'

Lemke sat in silence for a few moments, and when he finally spoke he was looking straight ahead.

'Tell them I can go much further. I can give them proof that the explosion was deliberate. With that information they could finish the Soviets. The people would hang them from the Kremlin walls.'

'You can pass this proof to me?'

'Of course. But I want the pension doubled for that.'

Boyle tried to hide his distaste. 'I'll ask them, Otto. Now I must tell you of the escape route.'

'I'm not going through any Berlin check-points I can tell you that.'

'You will listen each evening to the programme on Voice of America. Every day. When it is time to go, then at seven o'clock in the evening programme they will play a recording of a Beatles song called "Yesterday". In case you don't know it they will announce it before they play it, and again afterwards. Seven days from when you hear that tune you will go to Magdeburg to Steingasse forty-seven. You will ask for Herr Kopf. Herr Kopf will bring you over the border just below the crossing at Helmstedt.'

'There's minefields and guards all along that border for Christ's sake.'

'You will be brought across safely, Otto, I assure you.'

'They've discussed it with you?'

'Of course.'

'And you are satisfied?'

'Absolutely. When will you be leaving Moscow?'

'I don't know.'

'Can you remember the details?'

'Seven o'clock in the evening, Voice of America. Song called "Yesterday". Seven days later to Steingasse forty-seven. Ask for Kopf.'

'That's it.'

'When do I get the confirmation about the increased pension?'

'Can you give me the proof now?'

'No. I'll bring it with me to Magdeburg.'

'I'm sure they'll agree, my friend.'

'The film is taped to the front slat of this bench. I'm going now.'

'Good luck, Otto. I'll see you when you come over.'

'You'll be waiting for me and the girl?'

'I'll be waiting.'

Lemke got up and followed the path to where it ran alongside the Moskva river. Crossing the bridge he walked to the swimming baths where he had parked his hire-car. His brief-case and bag were locked in the boot and he drove straight to Sheremtyevo.

Even before half-time the floodlights had been switched on at the Dynamo Stadium. Boyle sat next to the girl, and Saratov sat on her left, alongside Machin and Evans. It was an end of season match, and there was a crowd of 40,000. The blue shirts of Moscow Dynamo reminded Boyle of the Scottish colours. At half-time the two favourite teams of Moscow were drawing 2–2; and in the interval Saratov had spoken in Russian to the girl who eventually turned to Boyle.

'Mr Saratov says that you might not know that the Moscow Dynamo club was founded in 1887 by two English brothers named Charnok. It was called Overkhovo Klub Sport, and then it was taken over by the Electrical Trades Union so they called it Dynamo Moscow.'

'What were the two brothers doing in Russia?'

The girl spoke to Saratov in Russian, and then turned back to Boyle, smiling.

'Mr Saratov says they were manufacturers with a factory just outside Moscow.' She laughed. 'He says they were "boyars".'

'What's a boyar?'

She waved her hands. 'Grand men, noblemen from centuries ago.' She smiled up at him. 'It sounds a compliment but is not really a compliment.'

Then the teams were trotting back on to the playing area again, and part of the crowd were chanting a word again and again as the referee looked at his watch.

Boyle turned to the girl. 'What are they shouting?'

'They say *Krasnaye, Krasnaye*. Sort of "red is beautiful". Because Spartak wear red shirts, and in Russian it is the same word for red as for beautiful.'

Boyle looked surprised. 'Is that a communist innovation?'

The girl laughed, shaking her head. 'No, it's just the language. Red Square is Krasnaya Ploshchad, it was always called that, even in Tsarist days. So it also means Beautiful Square.'

The match had ended in a draw, and they sat talking together, waiting for the crowds to leave. Saratov seemed amiable and animated, and he talked about the new facilities that were being introduced especially for the games. And even when Machin said that he had seen Adidas shoulder bags on sale with the Olympic symbol for twice the normal price Saratov had grinned, 'Ah well, we're learning – slowly.'

The girl had said something briefly to Saratov and he turned to the others. 'That's an important point. Women's hockey is to be an Olympic event for the first time in Moscow.' He turned to Machin. 'We will talk some more tomorrow about your points, but you must remember we have big problems in arranging the games. We are expecting 150,000 Russian tourists, 150,000 foreign tourists, 12,000 athletes and 7,000 journalists. And I have to liaise with twenty committees of our Ministry of Sports. Everybody is sure I am here to prevent him getting what he wants.' He shrugged and smiled. 'And in some cases it's true.'

*　　*　　*

Boyle had left the minute plastic cylinder taped behind the cistern in the first cubicle in the washroom in the hotel, and when he got back from the stadium he had gone there to check if it had been taken. It had.

By the time they finished their evening meal it was almost midnight, but Machin and Evans still hadn't had enough. There was a dance in the restaurant on the twenty-first floor and Machin had heard that that was where the action was. They left Boyle to his sober habits.

He bought a bottle of mineral water from the girl at the table in the corridor on his floor, and then let himself into his bedroom. The curtains were drawn and he pulled one aside to look at the lights of the Kremlin buildings. There was a plane winking its way across the darkness, and he thought he could just make out the two soldiers guarding the closed bronze doors of the Lenin mausoleum.

He walked back to the table beside his bed and picked up the bottle of mineral water and walked across the room to the bathroom. As he switched on the light a hand clamped over his mouth. There was the smell of soap and nicotine as thick, strong fingers pressed his lips painfully hard against his teeth. When his hand went up to pull the hand from his mouth, a strong arm locked around his chest, pinning his arm to his side. He could hear the radio playing softly in the bedroom. There were no sounds from the man who was holding him except the heavy breathing from his exertions, but Boyle sensed that there were others nearby. Then he was vaguely conscious of another man beside him as his head was jerked back and he felt a pricking sensation in his arm. The light in the bathroom seemed to grow brighter and brighter, and then, as if it were a dream, he was in the bed-room, and he saw dimly that two men were standing by the door. In the corridor were men in uniform, and he was not conscious of any feeling in his legs as he was shuffled towards a lift that he had not seen before. The lights hurt his eyes and he closed them to stop the pain.

Galitsyn's anger had spilled out over Mazarov who had barely been able to speak against the flow of abuse. When Galitsyn finally fell silent Mazarov said, 'We know the flight number, comrade, we can pull him off the plane at Berlin. There is still time before he lands.'

Galitsyn shook his head. 'No. Put a full team on him, bug his office, his home and the girl's place, and see that they report by radio every hour.'

'D'you want him searched at the airport?'

'Yes. A strong customs search on every passenger on his plane. Pull their stuff to pieces. Strip them. Put Vadim on to the bastard.'

Mazarov left as he saw Galitsyn's anger start to rise again.

Galitsyn phoned through to the Lubyanka and was told that Boyle would be unconscious for at least another five hours.

He undressed slowly and moved the camp bed so that he could reach up easily for the telephone. As he pulled the coarse blanket over his shoulders he felt another surge of anger. If they had the German they could have played one off against the other. Comparing the stories, breaking down the detail until one of them cracked. But all he had was the Englishman, who Saratov and his team had described as cold and formal, unsmiling and uncommunicative. And he had not the slightest idea of what the two of them were up to. They had checked out Boyle in London. He was a respected lawyer, and the embassy had heard rumours that he might soon be made a judge. What the hell would a man like that be doing with a German sportswriter. He had watched the film of them talking in Gorky Park a dozen times but they had made no physical contact. They had barely glanced at one another. Nothing had passed between them. They had talked, but not for long. But it *was* conspiratorial. There had been no greeting, no handshake. No good-bye. And the only sound on the recording from the long-range microphone had been birds singing and the nagging of the old 'babushka', with the little boys. The signal path had been distorted by the trees. But why had the German left Moscow so furtively. He could have him picked up in Berlin, but there had been enough problems with the East Germans about KGB pick-ups. He'd have to try to grind the story out of the Englishman before he started upsetting the East Berliners. They had complained too many times already about him. Accusing him of ignoring protocol and riding roughshod over their 'sovereignty'.

Boyle was still unconscious when Galitsyn went into his cell and Galitsyn looked down at his prisoner's face. It was a lean face, the skin drawn tightly over the framework of bones. The drug had affected the muscles around the Englishman's mouth so that his top lip was pulled back to expose strong, stained teeth. The skin was sallow and smooth, and the stubble round the jaw and mouth was grey. The hair was sparse, but it covered the scalp so that there was no effect of baldness.

Galitsyn reached forward and felt the cloth of the jacket. It was good material and the clothes well-made. There was a label inside the jacket that said 'Simpsons of Piccadilly'.

He pulled the cell door to behind him as he left, and walked slowly to the control office. He had booked one of the medium-sized interrogation rooms, and he picked up Boyle's case, and the cardboard box of oddments from his hotel room and the pockets of his clothes.

Room 109 was about 15 metres square with a long table in one corner and a smaller old-fashioned oak table in the middle of the room. On one side of the table was a primitive wooden chair, and on the other side a modern swivel chair of chrome and black leather.

Galitsyn emptied the contents of the cardboard box on to the long table. A razor, and three blades in a torn cardboard carton. An old-fashioned shaving brush and a plastic bowl of scented shaving soap. A couple of dozen paper tissues, a silver-backed military style hair-brush and a black plastic comb. A flat round tin marked 'denture cleaner'. Two linen handkerchiefs with the initials J.B. and a worn leather wallet. In the wallet were an American Express card and a

97

Barclaycard, that Galitsyn put to one side when he saw the word 'Visa'. An Omega wrist-watch with a steel case and strap. A creased photograph of a man and woman smiling at the camera as they stood on a lawn with a big house in the background.

There was a driving licence and an insurance policy for a Rover 3500 car. The passport was valid for another two years, and there was only one visa, for the current visit. There were the 'in' and 'out' immigration stamps for a transit journey through Amsterdam.

Two white terylene shirts, a pair of socks, a dark blue suit, a heavy dressing-gown, and a pale brown overcoat were the only clothes. Separately was an old leather purse with a few English coins, five rubles and a few copecks. Fifty-two sterling pound notes had following serial numbers and were still banded in twenties from a bank.

There was nothing incriminating, nothing suspicious; and that was suspicious in itself. Galitsyn pressed the button on the under-edge of the table and then wrote out a note for the duty officer at the KGB forensic laboratory. He handed all Boyle's possessions and the note to the orderly when he came.

He pressed the bell again and told the orderly that he was to be informed when the prisoner in 17A was conscious.

'He came round about ten minutes ago, comrade colonel. Just after you left his cell.'

'Bring him to me in ten minutes.'

Galitsyn sat in the swivel chair with his eyes closed. If they had not known of the German's intention to defect, no suspicion would have fallen on Boyle. Was Boyle some contact for the German's defection to England. But what could the German know that would interest the West. A sportswriter had no secrets. And why should a lawyer be his contact. The thin file on Boyle showed that he was fully occupied with the law. He was continuously in court when the courts were sitting. Could it be something simple like the German bolting to London to work as a TV sports journalist, and Boyle was negotiating terms. But if that were the case, why the elaborate and furtive meeting in Moscow. The information they had on the two men showed no possible interest that they could have in common.

Then the door opened, and a guard pushed Boyle into the room. His feet were bare and he walked unsteadily although he walked with his chin up, trying to focus his eyes on Galitsyn.

Galitsyn pointed to the chair. 'Sit down.'

Boyle sat down unsteadily, and he kept his hands on the table as if to keep his balance. With obvious effort Boyle lifted his eyes to look at Galitsyn.

'Why,' his voice trembled, 'have I been assaulted and brought here?'

'You are James Boyle of "The Sheiling", Limpsfield, Surrey, England?'

'I am.'

'Why are you in Moscow?'

'I am here to . . .' Boyle's eyes closed and he swallowed as if he needed air ' . . . to advise the TV team on legal matters.'

'For no other reason?'

Boyle's eyes opened and Galitsyn saw that his right hand was trembling on the desk top.

'What offence am I charged with?'

'Answer my question.'

'What offence am I charged with?'

Galitsyn noted the evasion and wondered why a simple denial had not been enough.

'Are you a homosexual, Boyle?'

'Good God no. Why should you ask that?'

'You are not married according to the reports I have received, you appear to have no relationships with women.'

'Neither do Roman Catholic priests.'

Galitsyn half smiled. 'I shouldn't rely on that, Mr Boyle.' He was silent for a few moments to let Boyle absorb the fact that they had checked his background. And he noted too that where Boyle was sure of his ground there was no evasion in his answer. His response was always a quick denial.

99

'Is the TV company a client of yours.'

'I am a barrister, I don't have clients. I am briefed by solicitors.'

Galitsyn was an experienced interrogator and he had sensed already that this man had pride in his integrity. That must be the first objective. To break down that pride.

'When did you arrive in Moscow?'

'On Friday.'

'You say you are briefed by solicitors for your work.'

'Yes.'

'What is the name of the solicitor who briefed you to come to Moscow?'

There was a long pause, and then Boyle said, 'It was a solicitor working for a government department.'

'Why should a government solicitor be interested in the legal affairs of a commercial company?'

'Because these particular matters are, in a way, between the two governments.'

'But you told comrade Saratov that both the BBC and your own company were quite independent of the government.'

'That is correct.'

'So I ask you again, why should a government solicitor be concerned with a normal commercial contract between your independent company and an independent Soviet company?'

'There are diplomatic aspects.'

'Tell me.'

'The government will be concerned that everything is done to ensure a successful outcome.'

'Do they not trust your negotiating team?'

'Of course they do.'

'So why does a government solicitor think it is necessary to brief a barrister. Why do they not leave it to the company to choose their own man?'

'I suppose it was felt to be important.'

'Do the TV company have their own solicitors?'

'I'm sure they do.'

'Who are they?'

'I don't know.'

'You didn't consult with them before you came to Moscow?'

'No.'

Galitsyn pressed the bell under the desk top and stood up.

'You are lying, Boyle.' He nodded to the guard who had opened the door. 'Take him back.'

In the customs shed at Schönefeld the seventeen passengers on the LOT flight from Moscow complained, threatened, and abused, as their luggage and its contents were gone over inch by inch, but the officials made neither apologies nor explanations. And when they were led away for individual body-searches, those whose turn was to come stood in a silent group waiting for their names to be called.

When it was Lemke's turn and he was stripped, the official went over him slowly and methodically, slipping on a thin rubber glove to check his anus and handle his scrotum. Then he was X-rayed. His head and the whole of his body. They made him wait for the X-ray film to be developed and it was three hours before he let himself into his office. He sat down with a whisky, and it was an hour before he pulled himself together enough to phone the girl. Her voice was thick with sleep but he told her to call a taxi and come over. In a couple of hours she said. But he said no, she should come right away. He felt sure she was not alone. Probably that bastard Karl, or some foreigner she had picked up in the 'Budapest'. Maybe it would be more sensible to leave her behind. There would be girls enough in the States. Girls who didn't open their legs for twenty dollars when he was away.

But when the bell rang, and he let her in, all those thoughts melted away. Only in the dreariness of East Berlin would he get a girl so beautiful. She had laughed at his impatience but in the bedroom she had responded to his urgent lust with an eagerness that matched his own; her lips against his ear urging him to have her again and again. And when finally he was still, and she asked him how he had got on in

Moscow, he had wondered for a moment what she was talking about.

He rolled off her, reaching for his cigarettes and lighter. He lit a cigarette for her and then one for himself.

'D'you still want to go with me, Ushi?'

She turned to look at his face. 'Of course.'

'Then there are things we must do.'

'What things?'

'We must decide what we can sell. We can't sell much or people will be suspicious. And we must buy jewellery – good stuff. Small stuff. Gold and diamonds.'

'What about your typewriter and the rest of the office stuff?'

'We'll have to leave all that.'

'When are we going, Otto?'

'Soon. Very soon.'

'Is it fixed like you wanted?'

'Yes.'

'And they know about me?'

'Yes. You're part of the deal.'

'Tell me where we're going, Otto.'

He looked at her face. She was so beautiful, but she was stupid too. Feckless. But her hand was doing exciting things to him and she was smiling up at him. 'Tell me, Otto. Before you do it to me again.'

He pulled her to him, and as her leg went over him he said, 'To the United States. We're going to live in the United States.'

Machin and Evans breakfasted alone and then went to Boyle's room. There was no answer to their knocking and when they tried the door it was locked.

At the reception desk they asked if there was a message, but there was nothing.

By midday they had had no contact from the Intourist girl or from Saratov, and they tried Boyle's room again. This time the door opened. There were no signs of Boyle. No clothes in the wardrobe. Nothing in the bathroom. The

102

room had been cleaned and was ready for a new guest.

They took the elevator down to the foyer without speaking. Everything looked so normal. People coming through the big glass doors, others standing in small groups laughing and chatting, new arrivals booking in at reception, and porters carrying luggage from taxis.

Machin reached into his inside pocket for his diary and found the list his secretary had typed out for him. It was at the top of the list. British Embassy tel. 231-95-55. He had been warned that the lines would be tapped. He turned to look at Evans.

'I'm going to phone the embassy, but the lines will be tapped.'

'So what. The bugger's missing. This is Moscow mate, not Cardiff.'

They walked over to the telephone canopies, and Machin consulted his list again. He fished in his right-hand trouser pocket where he kept his Russian coins and found a two copeck piece. He pressed it into the slot and heard the dialling tone. Then a man's voice with a Lancashire accent replied.

'British Embassy, can I help you.'

'We want to speak to the ambassador.'

'His Excellency is lunching at the French Embassy, is there anyone else who can help you?'

'I don't know. Is there a military attaché. Someone like that?'

'A moment please.'

There was a pause and several clicks.

'Dugdale. Military attaché. Who is that?'

'My name's Machin. I'm leading a liaison team from Independent TV and I want . . .'

'Ah yes. You want the Cultural attaché. I'll see if . . .'

'One of our team has gone missing.'

There was a long silence at the other end.

'When did you see him last. What's the name?'

'The name's Boyle. James Boyle, QC. We haven't seen him since he went to his room last night.'

103

'You've been in his room?'

'Yes. His stuff has gone. All of it.'

'I see. Hold on a minute.'

There was such a long silence that Machin thought that the connection might have been broken. But the voice came back again.

'What did you say your name was?'

'Machin. Terry Machin.'

'Where are you now?'

'In the Rossiya Hotel.'

'That's where you're staying?'

'Yes.'

'OK. You stay right there, Mr Machin. Stay by the reception desk. In the open, in public. Where you can be seen. Somebody will be over there in ten minutes, OK?'

'OK.'

Machin stood there looking at Tudor Evans. 'Shit. Why did this have to happen. Saratov will kick our arses all over the Kremlin after this.'

'What d'you think's happened?'

'God knows. Probably been caught in compromising circumstances, and they're going to screw him until he tells them the secrets of the High Court. What judges do when the lights go out. Oh shit.'

It was less than ten minutes later when the embassy man had hurried through the entrance and he spotted them immediately.

'Machin?'

'Yes.'

'Longridge. British Embassy. Where's your kit?'

'Upstairs in our bedrooms.'

'Right let's go up and put it together. And don't talk in the lift or in your bedrooms.'

Longridge sheepdogged from one room to the other, urging them on with a waving hand and one finger to his lips.

They had two cases each, and nobody stopped them as they walked out of the hotel.

'The car over there,' Longridge said.

The embassy driver loaded their bags into the boot and then they were sweeping into Ulitsa Razina. They recognized the Dynamo Stadium as they passed it ten minutes later, and then they were on the highway to the airport. It was Machin who noticed it.

'Is it OK to speak now?'

'Yes.'

'There's a car been following us all the way.'

Longridge spoke from the front passenger seat without looking round. 'Can you see the number-plate?'

'Yes.'

'What colour are the numbers?'

'Black.'

'On a white plate?'

'Yes.'

'Do the markings start with dash zero one?'

'Yes.'

'That's OK then, that's one of our embassy cars. Just a precaution.'

'Have you booked seats on a plane for us?'

'That'll be no problem. But you'll have half an hour to wait.'

In fact they had an hour to wait, and Longridge had gone off several times to telephone the embassy. When Machin asked him what was happening Longridge said, 'It's all under control. You two just get back to London. You'll be met at Heathrow by a Commander Shelley from Special Branch. He'll talk to you, and you'll be required to sign an Official Secrets Act declaration. You won't discuss anything about Boyle with anybody. Not your family, nor your company. Nobody. Understand?'

They both nodded glumly.

CHAPTER THIRTEEN

When Boyle was brought into the interrogation room for the second time that day Galitsyn saw that the effects of the drug had worn off. He waved Boyle to the chair again and sat down opposite him.

'Well, Mr Boyle. What have you to say?'

'About what?'

'About what you are doing in Moscow.'

'I've already told you. I am legal adviser to the TV team.'

'What else are you here for?'

'Just that.'

Galitsyn watched Boyle's face. Boyle had overcome his scruples. He would lie now without hesitating. They were adversaries now, and all he had to do was to find what areas Boyle lied about. Let him feel safe, then shake him. Let him recover, and then, when he was sure of himself, do it again.

'I understand you are an advocate, Mr Boyle. You generally prosecute criminals?'

'Yes. Not always.'

'And you prosecute on behalf of the police or the Home Ministry.'

'The Home Secretary, yes.'

'So you work for the State.'

'No, I prosecute for the State. I don't work for anybody.'

'But the State pays you. The police or the Ministry.'

'Yes.'

'So you work for the State.'

He saw the self-assurance in Boyle's eyes as he shook his head. And just as Boyle was about to speak Galitsyn interrupted.

'Who was your friend in Gorky Park yesterday afternoon?'

Galitsyn saw the shock and confusion on Boyle's face,

and there were long moments before Boyle answered.

'Who do you mean?'

'You admit that you went to Gorky Park yesterday afternoon?'

'There is nothing to admit. It is not an offence surely, even under Soviet law, to walk in a public park in daylight?'

Galitsyn noticed the 'even' and said, 'Who was your friend, Mr Boyle?'

'Just a man who was sitting on the same bench.'

'What did you talk about?'

'Has my embassy been informed that I have been abducted?'

'Forget it, Mr Boyle. The KGB and the Soviet government don't have to inform anyone about what they do. And you've not been abducted, you've been arrested.'

'Surely the conventions demand that they are informed.'

Galitsyn smiled. 'Mr Boyle you are a criminal. They will not be interested. You know that. They will say they have never heard of you. Why should they get involved in your stupidity?'

He saw Boyle lick dry lips as if he were about to speak; but he sat silent and still. A lawyer wouldn't like being classed as a criminal, especially when he knew it was true.

'You know where you are, Mr Boyle?'

'In a prison.'

'In the Lubyanka, the KGB's own prison for political offenders.'

'Do you provide me with a lawyer?'

Galitsyn smiled. 'No. And we are not very good at cricket either.'

He leaned forward with his arms on the table, his face a couple of feet from Boyle's.

'Boyle, I want you to understand something. One way or another you will talk. I assure you of that. Even young men, strong men, talk when they come in here. You are not young, and you are not strong. I *do* recommend that you talk to me.' He leaned back again in his chair. 'If not, I will have no choice but to make arrangements for you to talk.'

He banged his fist on the table. 'But talk you will, my friend.'

Boyle's hands were trembling again but his blue eyes were steady, and he said softly, 'You make your arrangements then.'

Galitsyn pressed the button and waited until the guard had taken Boyle away. He was quite a courageous old boy but he was beginning to lose his grip. A fish out of water.

In the central recording room he listened to the tapes twice, and then sat thinking, with the earphones pushed back from his ears. Maybe he should leave this to Mazurov. There were other things to do that were probably more important. What secrets could a sportswriter have that were so important. Almost without thinking he leaned forward, switched on the oscilloscope, and then set the tape-recorder to re-wind.

As he started the tape again he watched the screen of the oscilloscope. The display indicated a nervous speaker but when it got to the questions about what Boyle was doing in Moscow the line swept to a series of jagged peaks and troughs that only slowly declined back to the usual ragged norm. He switched off the two appliances and logged his use of the tape-recorder. He would stick with it until after Boyle had had his shot.

Sir George Fellowes, Her Majesty's Ambassador to the Union of Soviet Socialist Republics, was irritated almost beyond endurance. The Foreign Secretary had decided to make one of his lightning trips to Moscow, and was arriving with wife and entourage at Sheremtyevo just after midnight. The Foreign Secretary fancied himself as a breaker of log-jams, particularly where the Russians were concerned. He was certain that the fact that his father had driven a tram in Sheffield gave him an edge with the Soviets that a career diplomat could never have.

The present log-jam was the negotiation for classified computer software that the Russians claimed they needed for civil engineering. The Ministry of Defence insisted that the Soviets wanted it for weapon design, for which it was eminently suitable. Sir William would sweep in and, as he liked to put it, 'cut the red-tape'. The Russians would get the software, and the London Zoo would get an ageing panda. And His Excellency the Ambassador would be left, as usual, with the job of sorting out North Sea fishing rights, complaints about a BBC world service piece on Russian dissidents, a British Airport Authority squabble with Aeroflot about landing procedures, and now a bloody barrister in the Lubyanka. He would have to sit in Gromyko's office while some po-faced Russian handed round the usual snaps of some British oaf getting stuck into one of the KGB girls. Or, if fate was really against him, boys. As he bent to lace up his shoes he wondered again why they always went for blondes. Boys or girls they were always blondes. He had heard that the KGB made their brunettes wear blonde wigs when they ran out of natural blondes.

At the Kremlin gates the lights had changed to green and his official car had driven straight through, then down to the main entrance of the Great Palace.

The Soviet government were honouring the Polish Prime Minister. With troublemakers in Danzig, Krakow, and now Warsaw, he needed a build-up back home and the reception this evening was part of the build-up.

His Excellency spent his first hour in making the rounds, serving protocol as he was expected to do. Then his eyes went over the crowds to find Gromyko. He was so intent in his looking that he was startled when a voice said quietly, 'Can we have a word, George.'

It was Howard Kelly the US ambassador, an old friend from his days in Paris and Bonn.

'Of course. Let's find a table in the annexe.'

'Better we take a walk outside.'

Fellowes looked surprised, but he said, 'OK. You lead the way.'

Outside the building the guard detail was dressed in its Sunday best. Fellowes noticed that it was one of the

Khazakstani regiments, and the bland olive faces looked even more oriental in the light from the floodlights.

Kelly looked up at the sky as he strolled slowly with his hands in his pockets.

'I hear they've got your fellow Boyle.'

'Who's he?'

'Your chap. The one they've picked up.'

'Ah, yes. I hope to have a word with Gromyko. I assume they'll let him out in a couple of days. They haven't told me yet what he's been up to. But I'll raise a little hell as usual.'

Kelly stood still, looking at Fellowes with eyebrows raised. 'I shouldn't do that, George.'

'Why not?'

'Haven't your people put you in the picture about him?'

'He's a lawyer or some such thing. Legal adviser to some tin-pot TV team that's in Moscow about the games.'

Kelly was silent for a moment, tapping the ash off his cigar. Then he looked up at Fellowes. 'Somebody must know about him in your place or why did you bundle the rest of the TV team out so quickly?'

'I didn't know we had bundled them out.'

'They went on tonight's plane direct to London.'

'Probably just as well.'

'Boyle was doing a job. We're involved too. It's going to be a mess.'

Fellowes watched the soldiers walking to the gate, goose-stepping with rifles at the slope. He turned his face to look at Kelly.

'I wish to God they didn't just leave me to clear up the crash-landings. What the hell's it all about?'

'I don't know the details but our people have given it a top-security rating. It's CIA, not State.'

'Maybe that's part of why Sir William is on his way.'

'Could be. I suggest you don't make any inquiries at your level about Boyle. Let it stay at routine level. Third Secretary's about the mark.'

'What have your people said?'

'Not much. Just a warning to expect trouble.'

Fellowes sighed. 'We'd better go back in, and I'll make my mark with Gromyko and see if he smiles.'

Kelly grunted. 'If he smiles you'll know you're in the shit.'

Fellowes hadn't been able to make his mark with Gromyko but a senior Soviet official from the Ministry of Foreign Affairs had been a substitute, and he had seemed amiable enough. He hadn't mentioned the man Boyle. Kelly was a downy bird.

There was no window in Boyle's cell, just the dim light from a recessed fixture in the ceiling. Everything was concrete. Even the bed was a slab of concrete set against one wall. Only the door was steel, with its small inspection hole and a slider where his food was pushed in on to the welded bracket. There was an enamel bucket in one corner, that served as a toilet, with a roll of coarse brown paper on the floor beside it.

A whole day had passed without anyone speaking to him, although eyes had appeared briefly from time to time at the spy-hole.

He had occupied his mind declining Latin nouns and conjugating verbs. He had reconstructed three cases where he had prosecuted, to consider what had been the factor that tipped the verdict one way or the other. But gradually he had lost his sense of time, and slowly depression settled on him like a heavy blanket. His mind dwelt on the KGB man's threats. He had heard and read of the KGB's brutal methods, but what disturbed him most was the lack of procedure. He guessed he must have been already held for at least three days, but there were no formal charges. It was like some sort of limbo where there were no rules. Men could do what they wanted without thought of legality. He wondered if Lemke was in the same building. Perhaps Lemke was working for the Russians. There was a patch of rust on the door that was the shape of Africa and he stared at it, trying to remember the new names of countries' capitals. The west coast countries defeated him. He couldn't place Zaire or Angola and he realized that Botswana and Lesotho were just names.

When the guard came in Boyle was dozing, and when he was shaken awake he stood up lethargically, trying to collect his thoughts.

Galitsyn had had a further report on Boyle from the London embassy but there was nothing of great interest. They had checked the War Office first but it merely indicated that Boyle had been demobilized in 1945 as a General Service major. He had acted for the government in a prosecution against a Russian trawler captain who had fished in British territorial waters, but that had been as far back as 1960.

He looked up as Boyle was brought in, and left him standing for a few moments before waving him to the chair.

'Why did you meet Müller?'

Boyle looked puzzled. 'Who is Müller.' He had genuinely forgotten Lemke's new name. Galitsyn noted the frown and the confusion. It looked genuine.

'Müller was the man you spoke with on the bench in Gorky Park.'

'I didn't know his name was Müller.'

Galitsyn sat in silence. Boyle had looked genuinely ignorant but the meeting had been contrived, he was sure of that. Maybe there had been no need for Boyle to know the man's name. That was standard practice for KGB illegals when meeting a cut-out. But who was the cut-out, Boyle or Müller? And something must have passed from one to another. There were a dozen safer ways to pass a message, even in Moscow. But they had found nothing on Boyle, or in his bedroom and luggage.

'What did you talk about?'

'The weather, the games, nothing special.'

'In English?'

Galitsyn leaned forward as Boyle tried to decide what to say.

'What language, Boyle?'

'English.'

'Had you ever seen the man before?'

'No.'

Galitsyn was intrigued. The man told lies and half-lies, but there were questions where he lied only after hesitation or attempts to side-step the question. But interrogating like this would be a waste of time. He had too few cards to play. He pressed the button. When the guard came in he said, 'Fetch the doctor.'

The two men sat in silence after the guard had gone. Boyle looked at his hands on his knees, and Galitsyn watched Boyle's face.

Then the door opened. There were two guards and a man in a white coat.

Galitsyn said, 'Take off your jacket, Boyle.'

Boyle stood unsteadily, took off his jacket slowly and arranged it on the back of the chair.

The doctor slid back the shirt sleeve and looked at the thin bony arm. Then his finger and thumb found the pulse at Boyle's wrist and he stood in silence for two minutes. He reached forward and unbuttoned Boyle's shirt, pulling it back from his chest. He pressed the stethoscope against Boyle's ribs and listened. After a few moments he turned and nodded to Galitsyn who said something to him in Russian.

The syringe was already loaded, and without swabbing the doctor pressed to raise the vein, and the syringe slid into Boyle's arm. Boyle watched as the plunger was slowly depressed and the needle withdrawn from his arm.

At a nod from Galitsyn the guards left, but the doctor walked over to the corner and perched himself on the long table. That was the last thing that Boyle would ever remember of the next half-hour.

Slowly Boyle's eyes closed. Galitsyn looked at his watch and after two minutes he pressed the button under the table twice so that the recording machine was on a fresh tape. He gave Control another minute and then he leaned back.

'What is your name?'

'James Boyle.'

'Who is Müller?'

'Müller is Lemke.'

'How do you spell that name?'

'L-E-M-K-E.'

'Who is Lemke?'

'A German.'

'Why did you meet him in Gorky Park?'

'To talk, and take the film.'

'What film was that?'

'The film of the documents.'

'What documents?'

'Technical documents. I don't know what they were.'

'What were they about?'

'About the explosion.'

'What explosion?'

'The nuclear explosion.'

'Where was the explosion?'

'In the Soviet Union.'

'Where in the Soviet Union?'

'Chelya ...'

'Go on.'

'I can't remember, it's Russian.'

'Try. Try and remember.'

'Chelyavosk ... Chelya ... on a map.'

'Go on.'

'With railway lines.'

'Keep trying.'

'Binsk ... Chelyabinsk.'

'What did you do with the film?'

'At the hotel. In the washroom.'

'Where in the washroom?'

'First cubicle behind cistern.'

Galitsyn pressed the button three times. He spoke in Russian. 'Galitsyn here. Tell Mazurov to check that immediately.' He leaned forward towards Boyle and said slowly, 'Keep recording.'

'What did you talk about?'

'The arrangements.'

'Go on.'

'To go to America, but he wants more.'

'Wants more what?'

'More money, more pension.'

'Why does he want more?'

'It wasn't an accident.'

'What wasn't?'

'The explosion. They did it deliberately to find out what would happen. They killed their own people.'

'Who did?'

'The Russians.'

Galitsyn turned to the doctor. 'How much longer have I got?'

'About ten minutes. Maybe twelve.'

'Can you give him another shot?'

'Not now. It would stop his heart. In three days he could take a half shot. He's not young, Galitsyn.'

Galitsyn turned back impatiently to face Boyle.

'Boyle. Can you hear me?'

'Yes.'

'Was Lemke offering proof that it was deliberate?'

'Only if we paid more.'

'What did you say?'

'I said I would ask.'

'What did they say?'

'I didn't ask.'

'Why not?'

'I don't remember.'

'Try. Why didn't you ask them?'

'Something happened.' Boyle sighed softly. 'I don't remember. Men came, I think.'

'Did Lemke say how he would prove this?'

'The film of the documents.'

'No. How would he prove that it was deliberate. Not an accident?'

'He would bring proof when he came over.'

'When is he coming over?'

Galitsyn saw Boyle's eyelids flutter and open. Boyle looked at his turned up shirt-sleeve and then slowly turned his head to look at Galitsyn.

Galitsyn said, 'When is he coming over?'

Boyle looked puzzled. 'I don't understand.'

The doctor spoke in Russian. 'He won't remember any of it, Galitsyn. He thinks we've just this minute stuck the needle in his arm. He couldn't remember anything else if he tried. It isn't *in* his memory. Even when we give him the next shot you'll have to establish it all again.'

Galitsyn stood up, pressing the button. He turned to the doctor. 'Tell the guard to take him back when you've checked him. I must go.'

CHAPTER FOURTEEN

Parker stood by the window looking out over the centre of Berlin. Autenowski and Hamilton were reading the reports at the table. When they had finished Parker said, 'What do you think, Autenowski? Is he a plant?'

'If he was a plant why is he under KGB surveillance now he's back in Berlin?'

'Maybe it isn't surveillance. They may be guarding him. Cutting him off from us.'

Autenowski shrugged. 'D'you want me to send somebody over to check him out?'

Hamilton spoke up, 'The last film that Boyle put in the bog at the hotel was enough to nail down that there was an explosion, and we've got the first and second lots of material as back-up. What would be the object of a plant?'

'To make us publish the stuff and then expose it as nonsense.'

Autenowski shook his head. 'To do that the documents would have to be false, and they're not.'

'How do you know that?' Parker asked.

'We've got hold of an original from another source. I can't say how.'

'So what do we do?'

Autenowski said, 'We stick to the arrangements we made. If he doesn't turn up in Magdeburg we think again about how we use this material. If he comes over we de-brief him here. If he's been playing games we'll throw him back in the water.'

Hamilton nodded. 'I agree. We made a plan and we've got to stick to it. Even if Boyle talks they can't stop us using what we've got.'

Parker reached for the telephone, looking from one to the other. 'We're all agreed then.'

Both men nodded their assent.

Now that the main KGB building was out on the Ring Road they seldom used the conference rooms at Dzerdzhinski Square. But when a meeting was urgent, or it involved the old China hands of the KGB, the conference rooms were pressed into service.

On the top of the building the TV cameras were sweeping across the square, and knowledgeable passers-by guessed that Andropov must be expected at the KGB HQ. A few out-of-town visitors stopped to look up at the cameras and were moved on by plain-clothes KGB men.

Ten minutes later the big black limousine dropped the Minister for State Security at the main entrance. Galitsyn, watching from the conference room window, had seen the car and turned to the others who were seated at the table.

'He's here.'

There was Malik, head of the Second Directorate, Krotkov the head of Second Department, and Mazaurov. When Andropov came into the room they all stood, and Andropov nodded. He didn't introduce the man who was with him. He didn't need to, they all recognized Ivan Denisov, Secretary to the Presidium.

Andropov sat down at the head of the table and Denisov sat alongside Galitsyn. Andropov looked across at Malik. 'I hope this really was necessary, Malik.'

Malik said quietly, 'I think you will agree that it is, comrade Minister. Shall we start?'

Andropov nodded, and Krotkov nodded at Galitsyn, who took a deep breath and started.

'I've been investigating . . .'

'Who are you?'

'Galitsyn. Lieutenant-Colonel Second Directorate, comrade Minister.'

'How long have you been with KGB?'

'Ten years two months, comrade minister.'

'Carry on.' Andropov approved the two months bit.

'I had information that a German sportswriter was about to defect and I ordered a surveillance that . . .'

Andropov said testily, 'Don't talk like a policeman, Colonel. Just tell me the basics.'

Galitsyn started again, his chronological explanation in shreds. 'The German came to Moscow and he had a meeting with an Englishman named Boyle. I took Boyle into . . . we picked up Boyle, and under therapy he revealed that the German had passed him documents that indicated that there had been a nuclear explosion in Chelyabinsk. He gave this information in return for a pension and residence in the United States. He also informed Boyle that he could prove that the Soviet authorities had exploded a nuclear device deliberately to test the results. That we had deliberately killed Soviet citizens.'

Andropov sat in silence after Galitsyn had stopped speaking. He was looking towards the high windows but his eyes were focused far away. He was silent for a long while and then he turned to look at Malik.

'What do you propose to do, Viktor?' His voice hard-edged.

'We haven't intercepted the material so we assume that it has passed outside our control. The German left Moscow before we were aware of his connection with the Englishman. He is under a twenty-four hour surveillance in East Berlin. The alleged evidence of a deliberate explosion could be anywhere. Whatever it is, there may be several copies. Films, tapes or whatever. If we removed both men we could still be faced with copies elsewhere. My own inclination is to take that risk and neutralize both men.'

'You say that that is your own inclination; is there some other inclination?'

'Galitsyn suggested an alternative.'

Andropov nodded to Galitsyn. 'Let me hear it.'

'There is nothing we can do to neutralize the information concerning the explosion. They will already have that, and will no doubt use it. But if we could prove that the explosion was not deliberate . . .'

Andropov's fist crashed on the table, his face deep red with anger. 'How dare you ... *if* we can prove ... do you really think we would cold-bloodedly kill our own people?' Both Malik and Krotkov said later that they had seen tears in Andropov's eyes.

Galitsyn shifted in his chair. 'Comrade Minister, I did not mean that there *was* doubt, I only put forward that it is difficult to *prove* a negative. The people on the spot were killed. Only they could say what happened. If it had been deliberate maybe there would be documented instructions, or somebody would have passed an order. When no such order was ever given there *is* no evidence.'

'So who do we try and prove this to? The Americans? The British? My God, would our *own* people believe us?' Andropov pushed back his chair and stood up. He turned and walked slowly to the windows and stood staring into the distance as the others sat silently at the table. Finally, he swung round and looked at Galitsyn.

'Go on, Galitsyn.'

'So far as we know, comrade Minister, Boyle and the German are the only people to suggest that the explosion was not an accident. And Boyle is merely the recipient of the German's statement. Boyle was arrested before he passed on this particular piece of information. What I suggest is that I am allowed to attempt to convince Boyle that it is a lie.'

'To what end? There's still the German.'

'He is completely under our control. His mail, telephone calls in and out, are monitored. He is under surveillance twenty-four hours a day.'

'How in God's name could you convince this man?'

'I don't know, comrade Minister. All I ask is that I am allowed to try.'

'He has no interest in believing us whatever we do.'

'Our London embassy say he was shortly to become a judge. He doesn't like even his own lies. There is a chance I could convince him if I was given suitable support.'

Andropov turned to look out of the window again. Without turning round he said, 'What if you fail?'

'Then we remove him.'

'Why not remove him anyway?'

'Because if we can convince him, and then release him, he can convince his people that it is a lie. There will be somebody over there to spoil their story.'

'They will say we have turned him.'

'Not if he has the facts. If *he* believes, *they* will have to believe. They have no reason to think otherwise. Their only other course would be to publish facts which they know are likely to be untrue, and knowing we have convinced Boyle they will assume we can convince others.'

'And the German?'

'It depends on how I succeed with Boyle, and what I can discover. In the end we eliminate him, but the timing is important.'

Andropov turned and looked at Ivan Denisov.

'What do you think?'

'I think you're all crazy. Just kill them both immediately.'

'And if the German has left his so-called proof in some place, and informed a third party to release it if he disappears or dies?'

'Find out if that is the case before he dies.'

Andropov walked slowly back to the table and sat down. He looked across at Galitsyn. 'What material has already been passed on by the Englishman?'

'I don't know, comrade Minister. He doesn't know himself. But his controllers were satisfied or they would not have continued the operation.'

Andropov looked at Malik. 'I must consult others on this but my own feeling is that Galitsyn should do this unless or until we can work out a better solution. Don't start this operation until I give you the order. Stay by the telephone for the next two hours.'

Half an hour later Malik called Galitsyn to his office.

'The orders are to go ahead with the first stage.'

'What stage is that, comrade?'

'Talk to Boyle. Tell him what you offer to do. Assess his

reaction. The Presidium are divided on this but there are no alternatives suggested as yet. If you feel Boyle would listen, and is not so ideologically set against us that nobody could convince him, then they might agree to let you go to the next stage. They have great doubts about the wisdom of this but we cannot stand by and do nothing.'

'What is their particular area of doubt, comrade?'

Malik touched the blotter on his desk as if he were reading some message in Braille.

'You must already see it, Galitsyn. Doubt that it will work, doubt that *he* deceives *us*.'

'So why do they let me go on?'

'The fear that the other side may already have the so-called proof, and the outside chance that Boyle could convince them not to use the false information.'

Galitsyn twice reached for the telephone, and twice drew back his hand. Then, as if the phone were a magnet, his hand reached out again, and this time his finger dialled the numbers.

'Malik.'

'Galitsyn here, comrade.' He paused. '*Was* there an explosion in Chelyabinsk?'

There was only a short silence. 'Yes, there was. It was not an atomic explosion and not a reactor incident. It was an accidental explosion of nuclear waste, and the actual point of explosion was Blagoveshensk. There are files on the incident available at GNTK.'

'Have I got clearance for those?'

'You've got any clearances you want, Galitsyn. If you call for specialists or witnesses just inform me if they are not produced immediately.'

Galitsyn made out a written request for a micro-film version of the Chelyabinsk files from GNTK, the State Scientific and Technical Committee. And ordered a micro-film reader from technical facilities.

Two hours later he started reading the Committee's summary. Most of it he could not understand but some of the facts were all too clear. The enormous explosion had sent radioactive dust and materials high up in the sky, and strong winds had driven the radioactive clouds hundreds of miles. 285 people had been killed instantly, 2,400 people had died over the following five years from radiation sickness, and thousands of others had been affected. Towns and villages had been evacuated far too late, and the whole area was still contaminated. The area was still closed to all except the scientists whose biological research stations had been set up on its periphery. It was admitted that the area was still the largest gamma field in the world.

For the last week in May it seemed very cold to Galitsyn. You didn't need to be a scientist to realize that men were now playing with toys they didn't understand. And it wasn't all that much consolation that the men happened to be on your own side.

Boyle was sleeping fitfully when the guard roused him and escorted him to the interrogation room. He sat down when Galitsyn pointed to the chair.

'James Boyle, I charge you under Articles 190 and 191 of the Soviet Legal Code, promulgated by the Presidium of the Supreme Court on 16th December, 1966, of disseminating falsehoods derogatory to the Soviet State and social system.'

Galitsyn saw Boyle's eyes come alive. The lawyer was encouraged by hearing laws quoted. He was on his home ground. Or he thought he was.

'What does that mean exactly?'

'At least ten years. In Kolyma.'

'When shall I be tried?'

'Sometime next year. You will be informed.'

Boyle sat in silence and Galitsyn watched him carefully. He had considered waiting for the right moment before tackling Boyle, but he felt now that there wouldn't be a right moment. If time were not a problem he would have let Boyle rot in one of the camps for months, and then work on him when his spirit was broken. There was no point now in breaking Boyle's spirit. Creating a threatening background was as far as he would go.

'What kind of cases do you prosecute in England, Mr Boyle?'

Boyle looked surprised. 'Mainly criminal cases.'

'Are the defendants always guilty?'

'Of course not.'

'So sometimes you lose?'

'I am an officer of the court, so is defence counsel. We are not there to win or lose, but to see that justice is done.'

'Is it possible for innocent people to be found guilty?'

'I'm afraid it is possible. It seldom happens, but it *is* possible.'

'Are such cases on record?'

'Several are.'

'Do you ever personally dislike the people you prosecute?'

'No. I am never emotionally involved with the accused.'

'Our embassy in London tell me that you were possibly going to be made a judge.'

Boyle was suddenly aware of the ramifications of the organization that Galitsyn represented. There was no formal question so he stayed silent. Galitsyn watched Boyle's eyes.

'If you were a judge, would it be possible to find a man not guilty who you found repugnant to you?'

'Judges do not pass judgement on men, but on crimes. Alleged crimes.'

'So if our positions were reversed you would be able to listen impartially to what I had to say?'

'Of course.'

'Even though I am an officer in the KGB, and a Russian, and a communist, you would listen to what I said and judge only the evidence?'

Boyle sighed. 'We swear an oath on the Bible in our courts to tell the truth. How would I know that you told the truth?'

Galitsyn half-smiled. 'I could swear on a copy of *Das Kapital*.'

124

'That would not satisfy me, I'm afraid.'

'What would?'

'I don't know.'

Galitsyn moved his shoulders to settle more comfortably in his chair.

'I want you to believe me, Mr Boyle.'

'Why? About what?'

'Do you remember me ordering the doctor to give you an injection?'

'Yes.'

'What happened?'

'He gave me the injection, you spoke to him in Russian and then you left this room.'

'After he gave you the injection it was forty minutes before I left this office. You were injected with a drug, a derivative of Pentathol. I asked you a lot of questions and you answered them all without hesitation and truthfully.'

Boyle's face was white and his tongue touched his cracked, dry lips as Galitsyn looked at him.

'There is nothing you could have done to avoid answering my questions. If it had been done to me I should have answered too.'

Slowly Boyle clasped his hands and pressed them between his knees to stop them shaking, but his legs were shaking too.

'You told me about Lemke, and the film giving the details of the explosion at Chelyabinsk. And you told me that he had proof that the explosion was done deliberately to gain scientific data. What you told me was true, was it not?'

Boyle made no answer. Galitsyn went on.

'Did you believe that it was deliberate, Mr Boyle?'

'It is possible.'

'More than possible, would you think? Perhaps probable?'

'Perhaps.'

'Would you believe me if I said it was an accident?'

'How could you know unless you were there?'

'I could bring evidence.'

'From whom?'

'Scientists, officials, people from the area.'

'They would say what they were ordered to say.'

'And I say what I am ordered to say?'

'You may believe what you are told.'

'I have read the official reports on the disaster.'

'They may not be true.'

'Would you listen with an open mind if I brought people to answer your questions?'

'How would I know that they told the truth?'

'Your experience. Your judgement.'

'I would need to understand the language. Even in my own country it is difficult. Only a Russian would know if they told the truth.'

Galitsyn sighed heavily. 'Is there any man in the Soviet Union whose word you would believe?'

'There probably is, but I don't know who he might be.'

'There is no name that you can think of? A lawyer, a scientist maybe. Somebody you have perhaps read about.'

'I'm afraid not.'

'Any category of person? An artist, a musician?'

Boyle half-smiled. 'Yes, there is one.'

Galitsyn said softly, 'Who?'

'A dissident. Perhaps somebody in this prison as a political prisoner. An older man. One who speaks English.'

Galitsyn sat very still. 'You really mean that?'

'I do.'

Galitsyn stood up as he pressed the button for the guard. 'I'll find such a man.'

As Galitsyn sat in the central control room and checked slowly down the list there was a thought that he kept pushing on one side. What if he found a man Boyle would accept, but after all the experts had said their say Boyle still did not believe. And there was a half-thought lurking like a roving animal at the edge of his mind. What if Malik *had* lied to him? What if the scientific reports had been one of those concoctions that the GNTK's KGB members put together

126

from time to time to suit one State requirement or another.

Then there would be no choice, Boyle would have to be eliminated. But that would be the least problem. Boyle's people in London would put out their version that the explosion was deliberate and provide whatever material had been on the film as supporting evidence. And then the holocaust in the Soviet Union would start.

He phoned for Saratov and the Intourist girl to be brought in to see him. While he was waiting he called for their files but there was no time to read them before they both arrived.

He dealt first with Saratov. He wanted to know if Saratov had gained any impression of Boyle's likes or dislikes, prejudices or interests. So far as Saratov was concerned he saw Boyle as an arrogant old man, aloof and cold. Beyond that he had nothing to say.

He was half-way through talking to the girl when she said the words that rang a bell.

'Yes he *is* old, and he is *aloof*. He's very like my father.'

Anna Grigoryevna Panova had been transferred straight from Moscow University to the KGB immediately after she had graduated in modern languages. A year later, at the time when she was being considered for further training, her father had been arrested. Grigor Panov had been a lecturer in history at the university, and a novelist whose stories of Russia in the bad old days were enjoyed by millions. The thick family sagas sold in millions. But there had been a sharp satirical piece that had not been recognized for what it was, before it was published in the *Literaturnaya Gazeta*. It had been torn to shreds the following week by no less than the chairman of the Writers' Union in a piece that was both critical and a warning. Two similar pieces in underground *Samizdat* in the following month had led to him being deprived of his union membership. A scathing letter denouncing the union had been smuggled out and published in the foreign press, and at that point Panov had been put under house-arrest. He was too well known all over the Soviet Union for him to be denounced and tried.

'Where is your father now?'

'Under house-arrest at the dacha at Peredelkino.'

'Do you see him at all?'

'Not regularly.'

'How do you get on with him?'

She smiled and shrugged. 'He is my father. He has great talent. And I love him. But he would tear up all that has been done for the sake of protesting against a few stupid bureaucrats who take *blat* for giving privileges. He is old-fashioned, that's all. And he has lived a sheltered life.'

'What's your security rating now?'

'Zero seven.'

'Would your father co-operate with me?'

'You'd better ask *him*, not me.'

Galitsyn looked at his watch and then at the girl.

'Let's do that.'

Galitsyn had swept into Kalinin Prospekt ignoring the flow of vehicles; pressing on until they were across the bridge over the Moskva, then down the broad highway until the big sign that pointed south-west to Minsk.

Almost 25 kilometres from Moscow a road branched off to the left, and with the car's headlights cutting across the pine trees in the darkness the girl guided him until they were at the two-storeyed dacha.

An old swing stood in the garden, and across the grass was a line of golden light from a ground-floor window. He recognized Panov as the writer opened the door, his eyes screwed up as he looked out.

'*Anna kak ti pozhivayesh.*'

'*Khorosho, spasibo, papa.*'

Then Panov looked at Galitsyn and saw the uniform.

'Father, this is Lieutenant-Colonel Galitsyn. He wants to talk with you.'

Panov opened the door and stood aside. He was wearing a pale blue suit with a white shirt. The girl smiled. The old man wasn't going to let house-arrest get him down.

Panov waved them to an old-fashioned settee with a pattern of poppies and cornflowers. There was a wine bottle and a glass ready on the table. Panov put down two more glasses.

'Anna, help your friend to wine.'

He sat sipping his drink as the girl poured out the wine. When they picked up their glasses he lifted his own to toast them.

'*Za zdrovye.*'

'*Za zdrovye.*'

'And what does the KGB want to talk about with enemies of the State?'

'I came to ask your help, comrade Panov.'

The older man leaned back in his chair, holding the wine glass up to the light.

'How can I help you.'

Galitsyn talked, and so did the girl. And from time to time Panov asked a question. Finally he looked at Galitsyn.

'You will kill this man if we do not go through with this play-acting?'

Galitsyn nodded.

'I warn you that if I think that you, or any of the people you bring, are lying, I shall say so.'

Galitsyn nodded almost imperceptibly.

'I understand.'

'When do you want to start?'

'Tomorrow afternoon.'

Panov looked at his daughter. 'Can you stay tonight, Anna?'

She looked at Galitsyn and he nodded.

CHAPTER FIFTEEN

Galitsyn drove back to Moscow and decided to sleep in the duty-officer's quarters at Dzherdzhinski Square. There was a message waiting for him, instructing him to telephone Malik.

The phone rang and rang before Malik answered.

'Where have you been, Galitsyn?'

'I went out to Peredelkino.'

'Why?'

'To talk to Grigor Panov.'

'Why do you need to talk to that criminal at a time like this?'

'Boyle has agreed to let me make a case to prove that Chelyabinsk was accidental. He wanted a dissident as some kind of interpreter and referee. He was escorted in Moscow by Panov's daughter. She works for Intourist now. I think Boyle will accept Panov. I wanted to get Panov's agreement.'

'Did he agree?'

'More or less.'

'The others have agreed to the second stage if you recommend it. The British lodged a high-level complaint about Boyle tonight. Their ambassador saw Gromyko. They're worried, Galitsyn. They hinted that the Foreign Minister would be raising the matter with the Prime Minister tomorrow. It means they are worried about Boyle. Maybe a good sign.'

'Maybe.'

'How long will you need?'

'I don't know, comrade. It's like putting on a play without a script. It seems quite possible that I shall not succeed.'

'That would be very dangerous for us all, my friend.'

And Malik hung up.

*   *   *

All through the night the Central Signals Unit at the Ministry of Defence transmitted the movement orders to certain commanders of Armies and Army Corps, as far east as Irkutsk, to Samarkand, Archangel and Baku. There was no such indication in their orders, but their deployment would leave them strategically well-placed for taking control of the key areas of the Soviet Union. Separate orders were sent to commanders of armoured units that would leave them in a defensive circle with a radius of a hundred kilometres around Moscow. Special units trained for anti-terrorist operations were withdrawn unobtrusively from Poland, Czechoslovakia and Hungary.

In the dacha at Peredelkino, Panov and his daughter sat talking until the first stirring of the dawn birds. The girl hotly defending the system against the mild but well-informed criticisms of her father. As he lay afterwards in his bed, his mind too engaged for sleep, he thought about her summing-up. That he was just cynical, a reactionary who preached that human beings would never change. For her the hills were lit with golden sunshine, for him even the hills themselves weren't there. He had once felt as she did, but all that had faded with Stalin's purges. The purges that killed men not for what they did, not even for what they thought, but for what they *might* be thinking. And killed them with the tyrant's standard cry – that the end justified the means. Once upon a time she had trotted with him most days in the pine woods, and sat silent while he drank coffee and talked in one dacha or another. And Brodsky had given her sweets as she sat on his knee, to keep her quiet while he read the first draft of his poem. Holding the paper out at arm's length and coughing between the verses.

> Mary now speaks to Christ:
> 'Are you my son – or God?
> You are nailed to the cross.
> Where lies my homeward road?
>
> How can I close my eyes,
> Uncertain and afraid?

Are you dead – or alive?
Are you my son? – or God?'

Christ speaks to her in turn:
'Whether dead or alive,
Woman, it's all the same—
Son of God, I am thine.'

And Brodsky had quietly slid away to Israel, but there was no Israel for the non-Jews; the Panovs and the Pasternaks. Just the retreat into their own heads. Why couldn't the young ones see that they had traded God for a psychopath like Stalin, a peasant-clown like Khrushchev, and a sick moron like Brezhnev. Would they never see. Would they never learn.

It was the sunshine at mid-day that awoke him.

Autenowski and Hamilton disagreed energetically with Parker who wanted the diplomats to put pressure on the Russians to release Boyle.

'There's no point, Parker. If they hadn't known *something* they wouldn't have picked him up. If you pressure them beyond the normal routine then it will confirm any suspicions they have.' Hamilton's tone sounded impatient.

It was Autenowski who settled the argument. 'I've had a signal from Langley that instructs me to hold off until they send me new instructions.'

'When did you get it?' Parker asked.

'About an hour ago.'

'Nothing more than that?'

'No. But I'd say that something has come up that puts a new light on it. I'll have to wait, whatever you guys want to do.'

'How long do we wait?'

Autenowski shrugged. 'I've no idea.'

It was not quite midnight in Washington DC, and the men around the glass-topped table were dressed as they had been when they were reached. Klingman was wearing white tennis

132

shorts, a white shirt and sneakers, Pardoe, from NSA, was wearing a well-cut tan coloured suit, and Christianson, deputy-director of the CIA, was wearing a tuxedo without a tie.

Spread in front of them were a dozen photographs and two buff envelopes stuffed thick with more photographs. Nobody was talking as the photographs were passed from one to another. Pardoe half-stood and reached for the single sheet of typewritten paper. He had read it before, but he read it again. It was headed 'Evaluation summary of Samos photographs 917–1200. Grids 17–45, Soviet Union, all latitudes, 22.35 hours, June 1 1980'.

When Pardoe had finished reading the summary he looked across at Christianson.

'When we contacted your duty-officer he told us that there might be some significance for your people. Is there?'

Christianson nodded. 'I think so, but we'd have to have a Pentagon view first. D'you want to wait while I get someone over?'

'I'd better.'

Christianson had telephoned General Kornfeld himself.

When he sat back at the table he said, 'Did your man who wrote the summary have any military background?'

'Yes. He was a Pentagon analyst before he came to us. A colonel.'

'Do the Pentagon get copies of photographs when you feel they're important?'

'They get them all, with two days' delay. But when we spot anything like this they get them right away. But no evaluation.'

'Why not?'

Pardoe smiled and shrugged. 'They are the experts, not us. We interpret photographs, but not the situation.'

Then Kornfeld was shown in by Christianson's assistant. He was wearing a khaki shirt and trousers, and looked ready to go on parade. The others greeted him, and Christianson pulled out a chair for him.

'Gentlemen,' Kornfeld said brusquely as he sat down,

nodding to them. Christianson leaned back in his chair to look at him.

'We'd like your opinion, General.' He waved his hand towards the photographs. 'These are the latest satellite pictures covering the Soviet Union. They indicate extensive movements by the Red Army. NSA also report considerable radio traffic on the military radio networks in the USSR. There's a summary here if you'd care to read it.'

Christianson slid the page along to Kornfeld, and they sat in silence while he read the report.

When he had read to the bottom of the page his eyes went back to the top and he read it again. Finally he looked up.

'How can I help you, gentlemen?'

'What do you think's going on?'

Kornfeld rubbed his big nose. 'Well they're not offensive deployments, that's for sure. We have had no information about exercises, but that's what it looks like to me.'

'What would you reckon the object of the exercise to be?'

'They are pulling troops away from their frontiers so it's not aggressive. It may be merely a communications exercise with troops, or it could be to test their plans for big city control after nuclear attack.'

'Would they use regular troops for that?'

'Depends on the scenario. You could expect major civil disturbance after the second day of nuclear attacks. We have made provision for that ourselves.'

'There's nothing else that this deployment indicates?'

'Not in my opinion.'

Christianson looked across at Kornfeld.

'Do we do similar exercises, General?'

'Nothing of this magnitude. We regularly test the communications network and once a year we involve small token forces.'

'Why nothing like this?'

'Well, firstly it would scare the civilian population out of its wits, and secondly it doesn't teach you anything. The conditions on the ground aren't comparable with the likely conditions after nuclear attack. We shouldn't learn anything. We have tested special units from time to time in disaster areas, after floods, hurricanes or snow. But it doesn't teach us much.'

'Why do you think the Soviets are doing this?'

'Whatever the reasons are, they must be political not military. There's no percentages in this for the Red Army; and there's no indication of Air Force involvement, so it's not a test of combined operations. I would say they've either got some problem with army commanders at a high level so they're splitting them up, or they've got some anticipated civilian problem. Maybe bad or unequal distribution of food – something like that. They haven't actually moved into the cities, they look like maybe they're sitting outside waiting for orders or for something to happen.'

After Kornfeld had gone Christianson looked at the other two. 'Pretty good, bearing in mind that he doesn't know what we know. It can't be food, of course, because they've covered cities in some of the food production centres that can't possibly suffer from food shortages. I'd say that Kornfeld's analysis confirms our own.'

Both Christianson and Pardoe looked at Klingman and it was Christianson who put the question.

'This fits your theory, George, that the explosion was deliberate.'

Klingman shrugged. 'To call my thoughts a theory is too much. It looks *possible*. Whether it was deliberate or not, they have gained a mass of information that will help them in civil defence, in weapon development, in military strategy and nuclear physics. We've seen proof of that in the documents from Boyle. There's a mass of information in there that'll take us months to sort out. If they think they're going to be exposed they'll already be taking precautions and assembling a rebuttal.'

'What do you think they'll do with Boyle?'

'God knows. But he must be better dead than alive for them.'

'And Lemke?'

'The same.'

135

Christianson nodded. 'I think we should inform the President.'

Galitsyn had driven down with Boyle in the afternoon, and when he had introduced him to Panov he had taken the girl for a walk in the woods and left the two men to talk alone. He had already given Panov a background picture of Boyle, and on the journey to the dacha he had told Boyle about the girl's father.

Panov had suggested to Boyle that they should sit in the cane chairs in the conservatory.

'You realize, Mr Boyle, that I shall not really know if they are telling lies. Maybe I shall have an impression but nothing more than that.'

'And your daughter?'

Panov laughed. 'She is a Soviet, no doubt about that.'

'What does that mean?'

'It means she is a Komsomol member and what they say is the gospel for her.'

'Will they punish you if you say they are lying?'

Panov shrugged. 'Maybe. I don't think so. Perhaps they will *not* lie.'

Boyle looked around the room. 'This is a very nice house, Mr Panov, where is it?'

'Peredelkino. It's a small community for writers. A great privilege to live here.'

'And they still let you live here?'

'Oh yes. I'm not really any problem for them. I speak against their privileges and the bureaucrats, but I do not suggest revolution.'

'They have told you about this explosion?'

'My daughter Anna told me about it. There were rumours early in 1958 but they were soon forgotten. Moscow lives on rumours. They come and they go. Some are started by the authorities, some by dissidents, and some just grow naturally. And some, of course, are true.'

'Do *you* think that the explosion was deliberate?'

'I would find that difficult to believe. I don't say it is impossible, Stalin had two million of us killed in the purges before the war. Our leaders now are not that kind of maniac, but ...' he shrugged '... all power corrupts, and there is power enough in the Presidium.'

'If your daughter thought eventually that it *was* deliberate what would her reaction be?'

Panov looked towards the windows where a row of silver birches shimmered in the slight breeze. He was silent for some minutes, then without looking back at Boyle he said, 'It would be traumatic for her. A battle between her upbringing and her current beliefs. I just don't know what her reaction would be.' He turned back to look at Boyle. 'Why is a man like you involved in these sort of things?'

Boyle sighed. 'I knew the German many years ago. I was just a messenger. He trusted me.'

'You were forced to do this?'

'No, not exactly. I was persuaded.'

'How do your authorities persuade an eminent lawyer?'

'Patriotism, I suppose.'

'That's how the KGB are recruited, Mr Boyle. Russians are great patriots too.'

'I take your point, Mr Panov. It seemed different in London.'

Panov smiled. 'And Washington and London seem different when seen from Moscow.'

Shortly after Galitsyn and the girl came back, a truck arrived at the dacha and Galitsyn explained that the truck would be the base for a small security detachment to be posted at the dacha. He said that Boyle would be staying there until further notice.

Galitsyn left just before six o'clock, leaving the girl to stay overnight. He agreed that Boyle and Panov could walk in the woods but one of the guards would accompany them at a distance.

They had walked to the top of the hill to the old church, and Panov had pointed to a house with a green roof standing in a field.

'That was Pasternak's dacha. He lived there while he was writing *Zhivago,* and he died there in 1960.'

He turned and pointed to three tall pines. 'He's buried there, by the pine trees in the cemetery.'

'Did he die naturally?'

Panov turned, smiling. 'Oh yes they wouldn't have dared to kill Boris, no more than they would dare to kill me. He was the Bolsheviks' lifeline to the people. They bring flowers for his grave every year.'

'I thought that *Doctor Zhivago* was banned.'

'It was, but that was only half of Pasternak. The other half was acceptable.'

'And you?'

'All my novels are acceptable. I write of the bad old days before they came along. That suits them. They object only to my criticisms of *them*, and my criticisms are mainly voiced in private. To be under house-arrest is no punishment for me. Since my wife died I was happy to be here. I want no passport nor residence in Moscow. I tease them from time to time, but most of the time they leave me alone.'

They walked back to the dacha, and Anna and an old 'babushka' prepared a meal; and as Boyle sat at the table he had a strange feeling. A prisoner, his life at risk, in an unfriendly country, he felt suddenly at home. There was a solidity to Panov that encompassed them all. They talked about London and England, and then Panov turned to his daughter.

'I see you got your teeth fixed, Anna.'

'That was over two weeks ago. D'you like them?'

'Beautiful, my dear. What *blat* did you give?'

'Bolshoi tickets.'

Panov smiled at Boyle. 'We have abolished money in the Soviet Union, comrade. We have *blat* instead.'

'What is *blat*, Mr Panov?'

'My daughter Anna has a friend who is madly in love with a young man studying to be a doctor at Moscow University. His sister is a dentist. Her friend and her young man want tickets to the Bolshoi. As a much respected employee of

138

Intourist my Anna has access to such tickets. So they go to the Bolshoi and Anna has her teeth fixed. Not bribery, just *blat*. The English have a wonderful word for it. I forget what it is.'

Anna spoke without looking up from the plate of green figs. 'Old-boy network.'

Panov pushed his plate to one side and leaned forward with his arms on the table.

'Could I talk seriously for a moment, Mr Boyle?'

'Of course.'

For a moment Panov looked down at the table, and Boyle was aware that Panov was a handsome man. His thin ascetic face was deeply lined, but they were lines of life rather than age. When Panov looked up at him his eyes were a brighter blue than he remembered.

'I wonder if you would allow me to say a few words before our friend, comrade Galitsyn, tries to convince you that his masters are pure as the snow in Siberia.'

Boyle nodded and leaned back in his chair.

'Galitsyn is not a stupid man, Mr Boyle, but there are things that he will not understand. The most important is a question of viewpoint. It will not be possible for him to realize that you see the Soviet Union as a war-like, imperialist country, whose people are controlled by the fear of his organization – the KGB. And I suspect that you also will not understand his point of view.' He looked to see that he had Boyle's attention and went on.

'Firstly, I want to remind you that before the Great Patriotic War – what you call World War Two – the Soviet Union had honoured all its treaties and commercial contracts. Scrupulously. Secondly, I want to remind you that the Germans killed twenty million Russians in that war. That was about half the population of your country in 1939. There is no family in the Soviet Union unaffected by those twenty million corpses. They are not just sad statistics for us. For hundreds of thousands of Russian families the war was the end. They never saw one another again. I say nothing of our cities razed to the ground. We have rebuilt

139

them. But nothing can heal those other wounds. For me, I never again saw my father or my mother. Altogether I can name you twenty-seven close relatives who were killed, or just disappeared. My daughter Anna has no family but me. No grandparents, no aunts and uncles – nothing.

'Because of this we do not object that billions of roubles are spent on our armed forces. We see that as insurance against us being attacked again. You will remember that we attacked no one. We were the victims. And that is why we occupy Poland, Hungary, Czechoslovakia and all the others. If there is an attack on us the first onslaught would be outside our frontiers. We like friendly governments in those countries, but they are not really our friends. We know that. All through history they have been our enemies, so we keep them under control.

'God knows how many men like me welcomed Lenin and Marxism as a chance for a new way of life for us all. It took time for us to realize that Bolshevism and Marxism are *not* the same thing. But even with Bolshevism there is nobody in the Soviet Union who is not far better off today than before the Revolution. Workers, intellectuals, we have a life. All is not bad.'

'But you have a dictatorship that rules with fear through the KGB. You can't say what you think, or travel freely, there is no opposition allowed. No democracy. You live in fear.'

Panov smiled. 'This is what I mean by view-point, Mr Boyle. You have secret police in England. Your Special Branch and MI5. They can bug your telephone, censor your mail, and all the rest of it. But *you* are not afraid of *them*, Mr Boyle. Their faces are like yours, they are merely men, like you. If they arrest people, or harass them, you approve. They have probably deserved it, you think. And you are not afraid because you yourself do not offend against the law. I am not afraid, Mr Boyle. Galitsyn is not a monster to me. He has a face like mine, he speaks my language. He is just a young man doing his duty. There are laws, rules; and if I don't stick my neck out I shall not get hurt. There are always men in every country whose temperaments make them agitators. Who see injustice in the laws, or inequalities between classes. You have many such men in England, and they are dealt with by the authorities. Your public see this as a protection of their peaceful lives. If crowds get violent, who worries if the police are violent too. Like us, you say "these people know the rules and if they break them then they suffer". We have the same attitude. But behind all this we are afraid. For us, the Great Patriotic War was yesterday. We are afraid that it could happen again, so our reaction against outside criticism is always extreme.

'We complain about the privileges that our masters take unto themselves, but we don't *really* mind. As long as we have peace then let Brezhnev have his stable of motor-cars. Good luck to him. A few, like me, complain when they will not publish something we write, or paint, or compose; so we are punished.' He smiled and waved his hand. 'And who could say this punishment is barbaric?'

'But you have no democracy.'

Panov shrugged. 'Let us ignore whether democracy is good or bad. Do you imagine that the leaders of the Soviet Union deliberately plan a bad life for our citizens? Of course not. So they make mistakes. They make too many cooking pots and not enough TVs. But nobody dies or starves because they don't have TV. And it is not so long ago, Mr Boyle, when dying and starving were the norm for our people. Maybe we are not so technically advanced in some areas as the United States. Who cares? In the year I was born there were still men alive who had been serfs in Russia. Not servants, but slaves.'

'You realize that in the West we see your armies and weapons as aggressive, not defensive? You don't need so many to defend the Soviet Union.'

'Mr Boyle. Germany, the German people, were told before they attacked us that the war would be over in months. That our tanks were made of cardboard. They attacked us because we looked weak. We show the world now that we are strong, we flex our muscles as a warning. We flex

141

our muscles in fear, because we know that the West would like to see us buried. You take pleasure from our failures. You rejoice for a bad Soviet harvest. If a man offends our laws and is arrested, you call him a prisoner of conscience. We have no friends to trust, so we take care of ourselves.'

Boyle said softly, 'Do you really think that the West would attack the Soviet Union?'

'Who knows, comrade Boyle. We just don't want to tempt you.' He held up his hand. 'Were you in the war?'

'Yes.'

'Can you remember where you were on the 22nd of June, 1941.'

'I was in England. I don't remember where.'

'Can you remember one thing that happened that day. Anything at all, no matter how small.'

Boyle frowned, then shook his head. Panov's fist crashed on the table and there was anger in his eyes.

'On that day, Mr Boyle, the Germans attacked Russia. Three million German troops invaded this country on that day. It has been estimated that on that day one hundred thousand Russians were killed. Men, women, children, babies. But you don't even remember the date. In the following two weeks the dead were over a million. A million, comrade; people, living bodies, butchered into corpses. Would it have been too much, comrade, for your countrymen to remember that date when it was all over. Maybe just one wreath, in one year out of thirty-nine, for twenty million dead.'

There were tears in Panov's eyes and he could barely speak. Boyle and the girl sat in silence until he had recovered. He half laughed as he wiped his eyes with the back of his hand. 'Now it's your turn, comrade Boyle.'

Boyle sighed before he spoke. 'I'll remember what you have said, Mr Panov.'

Panov raised his eyebrows. 'You don't want to sing the praises of Great Britain?'

'It seemed that we were doing a lot at the time, Mr Panov. It seemed too much. But I can say this. I don't think my

142

country has even yet recovered from the effects of that war.'

'Anna,' Panov said, trying to smile. 'Play us a little music. Something calm and peaceful.'

The girl stood up and walked over to the upright piano against the far wall. She opened the lid and then played, and sang as she played. And when it was over Panov turned to Boyle.

'You recognize the little song?'

'I'm afraid not.'

'It's "The Lilacs" by Rachmaninov. Anna's mother used to sing that to us when she was pleased with life.'

CHAPTER SIXTEEN

Galitsyn arrived early the following morning and set chairs around the table. Boyle had been placed at the head of the table, flanked by Galitsyn on his left, and Panov on his right. Anna sat away from the table by the window. As soon as they were settled in their seats Galitsyn called out in Russian to the guard who stood by the outer door.

The woman who came in was in her middle forties, stout but well dressed, so that her body had a homely, comfortable appearance. Galitsyn waved her to the empty chair at the end of the table facing Boyle. When she was seated Galitsyn spoke.

'This lady is Natasha Guryenka, she is a stage-manager working at the Bolshoi Theatre. In December 1957 she was an actress with a touring company. She was in Chelyabinsk when the explosion occurred. She was in a hospital for nervous diseases for one year because of the shock. I have asked her to describe to you what happened. And Comrade Panov will translate for you so that there is no misunderstanding of language. You may ask her any questions you wish.'

Boyle sat in silence as the woman spoke, and Panov translated, slowly and carefully.

'My name is Natasha Guryenka and in 1957 I was a member of Theatrical Touring Company number 105 with the position of singer and dancer. We arrived from Sverdlovsk at two o'clock in the afternoon and walked to our hotel in Chelyabinsk. We were to play there for two weeks. I was unpacking my costumes when there was a very bright light and then another light. Almost at once pictures fell from the wall and then the hotel seemed to move and there was a loud, loud noise like wind and guns. The next that I remember is the room in the hospital.'

The woman looked from one to the other and then spoke to Panov.

'She wants to know if she can go. She says she has told her experience many times and it upsets her.'

Boyle nodded. 'Will you thank her, and ask her how long before it happened the arrangement had been made.'

Panov spoke and the woman answered.

'Only two weeks before.'

'Who arranged them?'

'The Ministry of Culture.'

'What was the name of the person responsible in the Ministry?'

'Comrade Suslov.'

'Does she know him personally?'

'Yes, he is married to her sister, and he got her the job in the first place.'

'Thank her very much for talking to me.' The woman listened to Panov's translation and then stood up and nodded to Boyle as she turned and left.

Galitsyn raised his hand again to signal to the guard.

The man who came in was wearing a uniform and as he sat down Galitsyn turned again to Boyle.

'This is Alexei Sukhodrev. He is employed as operations manager for Aeroflot. On the day of the explosion he was flying near Chelyabinsk. He was then a test-pilot in the Soviet Air Force.'

The man spoke as if he were giving a military report, and even without understanding the words Boyle sensed the lack of description. The man was reporting the facts and nothing else.

'Sukhodrev, Alexei. On the day concerned in December 1957 I was flying a light aircraft from the airfield at Kyshtym. The flight was to test new radio equipment. At 15.09 hours there were two large flashes of light, the first one short, the second one longer. Immediately afterwards my aircraft was forced up in the air to approximately fifteen thousand feet. When I recovered, the aircraft was upside down, and both engines were firing intermittently. I got the

145

aircraft under control, and I radioed my base for instructions, but there was no reply. The sky was dark and I realized that there had been an explosion on the ground. I turned and headed for Chelyabinsk. The cloud was thickening and I turned west to get clear of the dust and debris. When I was clear of the dust I radioed several airfields but was unable to make contact. I was called by the airfield at Kuibyshev. I reported that I had insufficient fuel and was redirected to the airfield at Zlatoust. When I landed there I was ordered to carry out a reconnaissance flight in the area of Chelyabinsk. My plane was refuelled and I carried out the reconnaissance.'

'What did you see?'

'I saw an area of approximately seventy-five kilometres square that appeared to have been bombed. There were big fires in Chelyabinsk, and I counted nine large villages and two towns where the buildings had collapsed and I saw no sign of life. An Aeroflot Ilyushin had crashed about fifteen kilometres south east of Chelyabinsk and appeared to be burnt out. The railway lines east-west and north-south appeared to be totally destroyed and two trains on the Sverdlovsk main line were on their sides off the track. I was recalled to base.'

Galitsyn spoke in Russian and Panov translated the man's reply.

'I confirm that I reported sick one month later and was diagnosed as suffering from strontium-90 sickness. I received intensive treatment in the clinic at Leningrad for three years. I was transferred to my present duties at Aeroflot in a civilian capacity and I am still receiving treatment for radiation sickness. I attend hospital once a week.'

'What did you think had happened on the day of the explosion?'

'I thought that there had been either a nuclear attack or a rocket explosion on the ground.'

'Now what do you think happened?'

'I have not been told.'

'But what do you think?'

'I think a rocket exploded. One of ours.'

When the man had gone Galitsyn looked at Boyle.

'The last person for you to see this morning is a nuclear scientist who was working at the nuclear site at Chelyabinsk on the day of the explosion. He was not on the permanent staff there, he was on a visit from Moscow. He is still on the University staff but not working on nuclear physics. He was the only survivor at the atomic plant on that day, and in addition he received extensive burns. There has been no satisfactory explanation for how he survived, but the theory is that he was protected by the steel doors of the building he was just entering.'

'Why isn't he working on nuclear physics?'

'When he was able to talk he said that the explosion was the fault of bureaucrats in the Ministry of Science, and that he had given many verbal warnings about the storage of nuclear waste at Chelyabinsk. It became a neurotic obsession with him, and he was eventually transferred to the laser research team as a mathematician.'

The man who came in would have been tall if it had not been for his stoop, and the lifeless arm that kept his left shoulder at a sickening angle. Three quarters of his face was smooth like wax, where plastic surgery had restored some semblance of features. His right hand slowly pushed back his thin straggling hair as he sat looking at them. Galitsyn set him off, and it seemed to Boyle an agonizingly long time before Panov started translating.

'My name is Viktor Pashkovsky. Professor at Moscow University. The new buildings. The ones on the Lenin Hills. I warned them many times but they didn't listen. Not one of them. They even had the infernal impudence to reprimand me. It was not my business, they said. So whose business were the dead? One hundred and nineteen staff died to save the faces of the bureaucrats. But the day. You want to know about the day. There were dogs barking and then suddenly they were quiet. Everything was quiet. It was like the end of a concert before they applaud. Or the end of the world. And the whole earth moved. Not just a lateral movement. It came up like a horse rearing up. I was reaching for the door and as my hand touched the handle there was the flash. As if I had pressed a button. And then the long secondary flash, and I knew. In that second I knew. And I could smell my flesh. The smell of roast pork. And then it was dark.' He paused, and then said softly, 'No more. I remember no more. But I think. Always I think ... every day ... many times. Those bureaucrats.'

'What do you think caused the explosion, Professor?'

'The nuclear waste. Just that.'

'What do you think happened?'

'Who knows? That is why I warned them. We had no experience of storing nuclear waste underground. They buried it as if it was household garbage. It's in containers, they said. Shielded containers. No possible risk of contamination. I told them. It's not just contamination, it's a question of explosion. Soil temperature, soil chemistry, seismic disturbance, we knew nothing of the effect of these things. Absolutely nothing. And, by God, we still know nothing. We know it's not safe now. But we don't know why.'

'What do you *think* it was?'

Pashkovsky whistled through his teeth as he sat thinking and it was several minutes before he spoke.

'I don't know, my friend. I just don't know.'

Galitsyn had left the girl, left her father and Boyle to eat together, and had himself eaten with the guests. As he ate he looked through the list of people he had arranged to present to Boyle. He would give the Englishman the chance to interview anybody he wished after he had gone through his own selection.

In the dacha Panov had been interested in Boyle's reactions to the people they had seen that morning. Boyle had made some notes and Panov wondered what had interested him. But Boyle had avoided Panov's questions, and had talked about Scotland, and his colleagues in the courts.

It was nearly three o'clock when they all sat round the table again.

'The next witness is a journalist working for the Tass Agency. He speaks good English, and he has been to the area on several occasions. He was sent there to write a film-script about the disaster.'

The man who came in was wearing a well-cut grey suit and he had the self-confident air of a man who was used to dealing with foreigners. His smile was faintly condescending, and he touched his tie as he started to speak. He spoke in excellent English with an American accent.

'My name is Alexander Vysotski and I am a feature writer on American affairs for the Tass Agency. I was twenty-five at the time of the accident in Chelyabinsk. At that time I was a reporter for the Novosti Press Agency and ...'

Panov interrupted. 'Novosti Press Agency is controlled by the KGB.'

Vysotski looked angrily at Panov. 'Rubbish, comrade Panov. You know nothing about these things.'

Boyle said quietly, 'Are you a member of the KGB, Mr Vysotski?'

'Of course not.'

Boyle leaned forward. 'Would you answer me – yes or no.'

Boyle saw Vysotski's eyes dart towards Galitsyn before he answered. Galitsyn's face was impassive. Vysotski adjusted the knot of his tie with casual indifference.

'No, I am not a member of the KGB.'

'Carry on, Mr Vysotski,' said Boyle.

'When I first visited Chelyabinsk I had been told to look at the area and talk with survivors so that I could produce a synopsis for a film. I did the research and wrote the synopsis after I returned to Moscow. I have visited the area twice since then.'

Vysotski looked down at his knees and brushed off imaginary specks from his trousers. He had said his piece and was now more interested in the state of his clothes.

149

There was only a slight edge to Boyle's voice. 'Was the film ever produced?'

'No.'

'Why not?'

'You must ask SovFilm. I merely wrote a synopsis.'

'What approach did your synopsis suggest?'

'I don't remember.'

'You have a copy, Mr Vysotski?'

'No.'

Galitsyn said something to Vysotski in Russian. His voice sharp with anger. Panov smiled but did not translate what had been said.

Vysotski looked at Boyle. 'Anything else you want to ask?'

'Yes. What was the purpose of your other two visits?'

'The first was to escort a party of scientists to the biological laboratories that have been set up just outside the area. And the second was to escort two official photographers to the area.'

'What kind of photographers?'

'One worked for Novosti, and the other worked for a ministry.'

'Can you remember the name of the photographer from the ministry?'

'Of course. Jacob Khudenko.'

'Could you describe what he looks like?'

'Of course, he is . . .'

Boyle put up his hand. 'That's all right, Mr Vysotski.'

Galitsyn looked at Boyle's face and was the only one there who knew where Boyle's questions were leading.

'What ministry did Mr Khudenko work for?'

Vysotski flushed as he realized that he had been trapped. He looked defiantly at Boyle.

'I don't remember.'

'You remember the occasion, you remember his name, you can describe him. But you can't remember what ministry he worked for?'

'No.'

'What did he photograph?'

150

'Buildings.'

'What buildings?'

'Temporary structures.'

Boyle leaned back in his chair.

'Colonel Galitsyn, I think this gentleman is wasting our time. He doesn't want to answer my questions.'

Galitsyn sighed heavily. 'Mr Boyle, he is trying *not* to tell you that model buildings were constructed in the area to confuse the interpreters of photographic reconnaissance pictures. The buildings were constructed to give the impression that the area was inhabited.'

'Was it inhabited?'

'No. It is still not inhabited.'

'Thank you.' Boyle put his head on one side as he looked at Vysotski. There were both criminals and barristers in London who would have recognized the gesture.

'I'd like to ask you just one more question, Mr Vysotski.'

'Yes.'

'*Are* you a member of the KGB?'

Vysotski's angry look went from Galitsyn to Panov, and finally to Boyle.

'I am not.'

'Thank you, sir. I have no more questions for you.'

When Vysotski had left they sat in silence, Panov staring at Galitsyn who was carefully examining the backs of his hands. Then Galitsyn spoke.

'I apologize, Mr Boyle. Vysotski is a major in the KGB. I was pressed to include him on my list. There are no others like him.'

'They wanted me to ask him about his interviews with survivors, yes?'

'Yes.'

'KGB or not, I would not have been impressed with his testimony.'

Boyle tactfully refrained from thanking Panov for his intervention.

'Is there anybody else you would like to interview, Mr Boyle?'

'I think perhaps there is, Colonel. I imagine that Professor Pavchovsky was not the only scientist who protested about storing nuclear waste underground.'

'There were a number mentioned in the records.'

'Have any of them been punished by jail sentences or put in punitive hospital conditions?'

'I know of only one. Lev Denichev. He is in the prison at Vyazma.'

'Why was he imprisoned?'

'He was in charge of co-ordinating all research on the effects of the explosion. After two years he put in a personal report that the explosion was caused by either criminal carelessness or was deliberate.'

'Can I see him and talk to him?'

'If it is possible, it will take me until late tomorrow to arrange. Maybe even longer.'

'Let's do that, Colonel.'

Not even during their evening meal did the three of them discuss what had happened during the day.

But when Panov and Boyle were playing chess as they sipped their coffee Boyle had led the way.

'What did you think, Mr Panov?'

'They must have been desperate to put Vysotski in front of you. I wouldn't judge Galitsyn too harshly in that business. He will have heavy pressures on him. More interesting is what *you* think.'

'There were things that I noticed. I am sure you noticed them too. All I will say is that my mind is still open. I am impressed by what has been said, but there is no evidence either way.'

'Of course, there is . . .' Panov broke off ' . . . no. I must leave it to you.'

'Tell me what you were going to say.'

Panov shook his head. 'Maybe some other time.'

It had taken two days and a Presidium decision before Galitsyn had been able to pick up Denichev from the prison at Vyazma. And on the car journey to Peredelkino the scientist had sat in absolute silence, refusing to respond to Galitsyn's attempts at conversation, and making no comment on his explanations of the reasons for the journey.

At the dacha when Galitsyn had introduced Boyle, Panov and his daughter, Denichev had nodded to each one in turn and when they were all seated at the table Denichev spoke for the first time. Looking at Galitsyn he said, 'I have no intention of talking while you are here, comrade.' He spoke in good English.

Panov said something in Russian and Denichev answered in English with a shake of his head.

'It doesn't interest me, *gospodin*. The KGB is the KGB, and I would not lift a hand to help them, even if I could. It is unlikely that I can help anyway.'

He sat there motionless, his face impassive, his eyes focused on some far-away horizon.

Galitsyn hesitated for a moment and then, his face flushed with anger, he stood up and walked through to the living-room and out through the door to where the guards were standing.

Boyle, watching Denichev's face, noticed the waxy pallor and the red-rimmed eyes that were half-closed as if the daylight were too harsh. And they were all aware of the clean white bandage round the man's neck. Boyle spoke very quietly.

'Would you like some food before we talk, Professor?'

Denichev shook his head.

'Some wine perhaps?'

Denichev turned his head to look at Boyle. 'You are the Englishman?'

'A Scot actually, but it doesn't matter. I was hoping you could help me.'

'To do what?'

'To establish if the explosion at Chelyabinsk was intentional or not.'

'It depends on how you define intentional. If you mean did some idiot in Moscow order somebody to press a button, then the answer in my opinion is "no". But if you mean did some moron who knew nothing about nuclear physics order the storage of nuclear waste in conditions that a first-year university student of languages could have told him was dangerous, then the answer is "yes".'

Boyle raised his eyebrows. 'Surely one could be the cover for the other.'

Denichev sighed deeply, then spoke very slowly. '*That* had not entered my mind. You mean that somebody could have put the moron in charge of nuclear-waste disposal knowing that it would almost certainly be unsafe?'

'Yes.'

Denichev turned to look at Panov, 'I couldn't believe that, Panov. Could you?'

Panov sighed. 'I'm an old man, Professor. Old men can believe anything.'

'My God,' Denichev said slowly. 'My God. It's possible.' Then he shook his head. 'No. It's not possible.'

Boyle said, 'You mean that it is not possible scientifically or not possible to believe?'

'Holy God, it's possible scientifically. It's happened. But what monster could *make* it happen. All my complaints were about stupidity, carelessness, not a nightmare like that.'

'If you had known about the method of storage would you have known that it would explode?'

'Oh no. All that I could have said was that it was dangerous. Leakage, contamination would have been my concern.'

'What caused the explosion?'

'Nobody knows. You would need to take that mass of nuclear waste and bury it underground again, in similar conditions of soil and temperature and containers, and wait to see what happened. So far as I know this is the only explosion that has occurred anywhere in the world in nuclear waste.'

'How is it normally stored in the Soviet Union?'

'It is stored under water on the seabed of the Kara Sea.'

'Did none of the people on the site warn Moscow of the dangers?'

154

'A few cautionary questions were asked, that's all. It would be assumed that officials in Moscow knew what they were doing. There was no history, no facts to go on. The reports and letters that I inspected were more queries than warnings.'

'In your investigations did you find any evidence of important party members or their relatives being kept away from Chelyabinsk immediately before the explosion?'

'On the contrary, three children of respected ministers were killed. One indispensable geneticist was so badly burned that he will never function again. The Minister of Agriculture himself was due in Chelyabinsk that day. He missed his plane because he was called at the last minute to meet a foreign delegation. His wife and child were on that plane. Both have radiation sickness and are partially paralysed.' Denichev shook his head. 'No. You would have to be a foreigner or a complete cynic to believe that someone ordered the explosion.'

'Did you believe Stalin's purges were possible?'

'We saw them happen, comrade. There was nothing furtive about those. The man was paranoid and there was nobody to restrain him. Those nightmares have long gone.'

'No paranoiacs today?'

'No. The lessons were learned. I've no doubt about that.'

'What about the psychiatric and medical abuse of dissidents?'

Denichev's pale blue eyes looked at Boyle's face, and his head nodded almost imperceptibly. He sighed as he sat silently. When he spoke his voice was thin and strained. 'And you ask me?' He sighed again. 'Let us be philosophic. The abuse of the dissidents at the most is murder. The other thing is not murder but slaughter, even ...' He turned to Panov and spoke in Russian. Panov shook his head and looked at his daughter. She said, 'Genocide.'

' ... it would be genocide,' said Denichev almost in a whisper. He put his hands palm down on the table as if to support himself. His eyes were on Boyle's face.

'I want to say to you, my friend, that I am not frightened

155

at the thought of dying. I am not fearful of the KGB or any other group of people in this country. So I say to you sincerely that I do not believe that anyone wished the explosion in Chelyabinsk to happen. Only a scientist could imagine how much information could be gained from this tragedy. No scientist would dream of making it happen. And I truly believe that no Soviet leader would entertain the suggestion if it were put forward. If you believe that such a thing could have been intended then I beg of you to search carefully your mind, and unless you could believe that your own leaders could do the same, then you should dismiss this German's talk as what it is – propaganda. Propaganda for personal gain.'

'But this man would be living in the United States, and if his story was false it would eventually come out.'

Denichev shrugged. 'Nobody will ever be able to prove what happened, comrade. That is your dilemma. And ours too.'

Boyle put out his hand to Denichev who took it diffidently. 'Is there anything that I could do to help you, Professor?'

Denichev half-smiled. 'Don't forget, my friend, you are a prisoner too. Only while you are here are you a judge. No. There is nothing that anyone can do to help me.'

Galitsyn had arranged for Denichev to be returned to Vyazma jail by two of the guard detail; and he walked in the early evening through the woods with Panov and Boyle.

They walked to the top of the hill by the church, and sitting on a low pile of granite blocks they looked across to where children were playing on the slope of the hill. It was warm, and the sun was still above the tops of the trees. Galitsyn seemed on edge, and finally broke the silence.

'And what were your conclusions, Mr Boyle, after talking with Denichev?'

Panov looked up at Boyle's face to see his reaction.

'Professor Denichev is obviously quite convinced that the

explosion was an accident. He blames ignorance on the part of bureaucrats in Moscow. But he says that the cause will never be proved one way or the other.'

'Does this convince *you*, Mr Boyle?'

'Well, the problem to my mind is that the bureaucratic ignorance could be genuine or merely a cover for something else.'

'Would you like to speak to the bureaucrats concerned?'

'What ministry do they work for?'

'No ministry.'

There was a silence and Boyle turned to look at Galitsyn. 'I don't understand.'

'They were dismissed and given prison sentences. There were three of them.'

'Where are they imprisoned?'

'In the eastern Urals.'

'There were a few minutes silence, and Boyle could hear a blackbird singing. A small breeze blew gently on his face.

'What do you hope will happen if I were convinced that the explosion was an accident?'

'That we should release you. Hand you back to your authorities.'

'And?'

'They will use the information that you have passed on to them from the German. And we shall admit that there was a small explosion twenty-three years ago, and we shall speculate as to all the fuss at this particular time. If they want to say that the explosion was contrived deliberately I think you might deter them.'

'And my arrest?'

'It will not be mentioned by us, and your people and the Americans will not mention it either. They would be admitting to espionage in the Soviet Union, and they would also be admitting to the operation being a failure.'

'And if they ignored my advice and it was suggested that the explosion was intentional?'

'Then the West could expect trouble. Real trouble.'

Panov looked at Galitsyn. 'You have a much easier solution than all this, comrade.'

'What's that?'

'You could arrest the German, see what his so-called proof really is.'

'And what if he has passed on his proof to others as he intended passing it to the Americans?'

Panov smiled. 'Mr Boyle was to be the contact. Let him make that contact. In East Berlin. He can discover what this "proof" is, and if others have access to it.'

Galitsyn sat silently, and Panov spoke again. 'Are you frightened of what you might find, Colonel?'

Galitsyn's head jerked up, and Boyle saw the fury on his face as he spoke in Russian to Panov. Galitsyn's voice was harsh and Boyle was surprised to see the anger turn into what seemed distress. Galitsyn pulled up the left sleeve of his uniform and Boyle could see the glistening livid burn-scar that covered his arm down to his wrist. After a few seconds Galitsyn let the sleeve cover his arm again. Panov seemed to be asking questions, and finally he put out his hand and gently rested it on the KGB man's shoulder. His voice was gentle and soothing, as if he were talking to a small child.

When eventually both men were silent, Panov turned to Boyle. 'Would you see Lemke in Berlin if that ended the matter?'

'What if I refused?'

'I expect you would rot in the Lubyanka for a few years and then be shipped out to one of the labour camps.'

'Is that what Galitsyn was saying in Russian?'

'No. What he spoke of was nothing to do with this business.'

Boyle shrugged. 'I seem to have no choice.'

Without making any comment on Boyle's remark Galitsyn stood up and walked away from them both, back towards the dacha.

As Galitsyn went out of sight as he took the path through the woods Panov turned towards Boyle. 'Galitsyn is very angry about the German. He sees it all as a continuation of the war. German propaganda forcing the Soviet Union to take action that could damage our security.'

'I can't see that it matters whether the informant is German or any other nationality.'

'I'd better tell you why, so that you will understand. When Galitsyn spoke to me in Russian he told me that he had had to watch while German soldiers raped his mother and then killed her. They did it in front of him. He was three years old when it happened.'

'Oh my God!' Boyle said, shaking his head as if to blot out the vision. 'How terrible. No wonder he hates them. It doesn't bear thinking about.'

'I'm afraid Galitsyn thinks about it all the time.'

'The sooner this affair is cleared up the better for all of us.'

Panov nodded. 'I shall miss you, comrade Boyle. I hope it goes well for you.'

That evening Galitsyn ate with them, and for the moment the tension seemed to have gone. They were a group. They knew about each other as soldiers know each other. They watched a football match on TV which was followed by a tour of the skyscrapers that had been built to house the competitors in the games; and 16,000 workers when the games were finished. But despite the relaxed atmosphere, Galitsyn switched off the set immediately the newscast started.

It was midnight when they finally went to bed, and Boyle sat in a chair by the window of his bedroom as his tired mind went over the events of the last few days again and again. He had gone from the deep depression of being a prisoner to a few days of spurious power with the scales weighted heavily against an independent judgement. And all this nightmare, the contortions on both sides, was because a greedy, worthless man decided he would like to come over to the West with his latest mistress. Cashing in on the cold war for an easy life, indifferent to the outcome. Maybe Galitsyn was right in his attitude to Lemke. But no doubt if it had

been the other way round then Galitsyn or one of his colleagues would be rushing to make some deal that would
embarrass the west.

He saw the first light of morning before he fell asleep.

CHAPTER SEVENTEEN

Autenowski read the message and then passed it across the table to Hamilton.

PENT INT. EV. SOV 49143

YOUR ATTENTION DRAWN TO AREA OF CHELYABINSK EX-PLOSION STOP YOUR REPORTS PLUS SAMOS PICTURES STRONGLY INDICATE PRIME DESTRUCT AREA PATTERN COINCIDES IMPACT PATTERN OF BEATEN ZONE TWO SS-20s. YOUR IMMEDIATE COMMENT REQUIRED STOP

Hamilton shoved the paper back to Autenowski.

'They've got their timing all wrong if our information is correct.'

'How come?'

'The SS-20 is a current weapon. They wouldn't have been developing it as far back as this explosion.'

'Langley put this suggestion to me last week. I think everybody's been looking for a sound reason why the explosion could be deliberate. Even that it wasn't nuclear waste.'

'Klingman's comments were enough I should have thought. He reckoned that it gave them information that would not be available to us until at least day three after a nuclear attack.'

Autenowski sighed. 'D'you know what?'

'No.'

'I reckon we'd better go over and lift Lemke. That will settle it one way or another. Everybody's trying to put together the jig-saw with half the pieces missing. Lemke's got the missing pieces.'

'Parker won't like that.'

'Because of Boyle?'

'Yes.'

'You've got to forget Boyle, or the whole damn thing will go down the pike. You ain't gonna see Boyle for a long, long time. And when you do it'll be at a show trial in Moscow. Another Gary Powers and the U-2 story all over again.'

Hamilton sighed. 'I'll speak to Parker and see what he says.'

Boyle stood on the lawn behind the dacha, his hands behind his back, looking down at his feet in an effort to concentrate. There were daisies in the fine grass, and it struck him that part of the trouble was that three weeks earlier he had never imagined daisies growing in the Soviet Union. The media at home had always gone on about Soviet citizens cut off from the rest of the world. Ignorant about real living conditions outside the Soviet Union. Victims of propaganda. But if a reasonably mature and intelligent man had never visualized a pretty dacha with a garden and daisies, or a KGB man who had moments of unhappiness, then who were the victims of propaganda. Was it only because he was a prisoner that made him wish he were staying with Panov? Why had all the pictures in the West shown dowdy women when there were pretty girls on every street in Moscow just as there were in London?

He turned as an arm went round his shoulder. It was Panov, smiling.

'*Do svidanya, tovarich.* They're waiting for you in the car. Anna's going with you. I'll be thinking of you.'

And Panov had walked with him to the small gate in the fence, and Boyle's spirits were low as Panov stood waving them good-bye.

Galitsyn did not take him to the Lubyanka but to the main entrance of the KGB building. The girl went off to an office on the ground floor, and Galitsyn took Boyle in the elevator to the fifth floor. There they walked down a long corridor to a room without windows.

There was a camp bed, a wash-stand, a table and four

chairs, and a telephone on a small table. On the bed were Boyle's bags. Galitsyn pointed to them.

'All your things are there Mr Boyle. Change your clothes if you wish. I shall be back with you in about half an hour.'

The call came through for Hamilton, and Autenowski sat watching him as he stood alongside the micro-circuit scrambler, listening intently. When he hung up he turned slowly to look at the American.

'Parker says our people won't go along with it. They're afraid that it might make things worse for Boyle. They may change their minds later on, but right now they're leaning hard on the Russians through the Foreign Office. They don't want any drastic action in case Boyle hasn't talked.'

'Oh for Christ's sake, they've had him for ten days, of course he'll have talked. If he hasn't talked, then pulling Lemke out wouldn't be connected with him.'

'They will have connected Lemke with him right from the start, otherwise they had no grounds for arresting him.'

'So why have the KGB put a round-the-clock surveillance on Lemke? And why did they let him get back to Berlin? Why didn't they pick *him* up too?'

'Maybe Lemke's a plant.'

'Our evaluation team at Langley have gone over all that. They say *he's* genuine and the *documents* are genuine.'

'We'll have to wait, Autenowski, unless your people can change London's mind on this.'

Autenowski stood up, his annoyance and impatience undisguised.

'I'll have to go back to HQ and check with Langley. I'll probably be a couple of hours.'

Autenowski never came back.

Christianson listened to Autenowski's report on the scrambler, asked a couple of questions, and then asked his assistant to trace the Secretary of State. Then he spoke to Pardoe at NSA HQ at Fort George Meade.

163

John D. Harrap, Secretary of State was attending a reception at the Israeli Embassy and Christianson had to wait almost an hour before Harrap strolled out to see him in the forecourt. He listened carefully but without apparently being impressed, and when Christianson finished, Harrap had looked up at the night sky, his hands in his jacket pockets. Then he crooked his arm to look at his watch.

'I'll see you in an hour in my office. Get Klingman there and Kornfeld.'

And without further ado he walked back into the embassy.

It was over an hour before Harrap arrived, and as he walked through the outer office he waved them into his own office and pointed at the oblong table. He sat down and loosened his tie.

'Now. Why are you consulting me?'

'I want to send in a team to pull out the German, Lemke.'

'Why? Why not go along with the British? It's their man in jail.'

'We think that the Russians might pick up Lemke.'

'So what. You say you've got the documentary evidence.'

'Yes. But he says he has evidence that the explosion was deliberate.'

'Do you believe that, General?'

'It has provided them with a mass of information that we don't have, Mr Secretary.'

'What do you think, Klingman? Haven't you got enough?'

'Enough to prove that it happened, certainly; but there will be much more. And if he has proof that it was a deliberate act to provide information, that is out of my field. That's political, not scientific.'

Harrap looked briefly at Klingman as if he were wondering if the scientist was being deliberately impertinent in his statement of the obvious.

'If it cost no lives, Klingman, how much would it be worth for us to do such an experiment?'

'Without the human factor it would not be worth doing?'

'How much, Mr Klingman?'

The scientist shrugged. 'Ten million dollars. Probably more. It really can't be estimated. Until you know the effects you don't know the value.'

Harrap looked at Kornfeld. 'Are their troops still in place round the cities?'

'Yes, Mr Secretary.'

Christianson leaned forward. 'I've just been speaking to Pardoe at NSA, Mr Secretary.'

'Who's he?'

'NSA liaison officer to the CIA.'

'Go on.'

'They have intercepted radio traffic from KGB HQ to a KGB unit in Peredelkino and it looks like Boyle has been taken there.'

'Where in hell is Peredelkino?'

'It's a village for writers and artists about twenty-five kilometres from Moscow. It's a privileged place.'

'Is Boyle a writer?'

'No he's an attorney.'

'So what's the significance of that move?'

'We guess he's been taken to a relaxed situation because he's co-operating. Talking.'

'How long did the British want to make up their minds?'

'It was open ended. They didn't even say that they *would* change their minds.'

'How long will it take you to get the German out?'

'Three days, four at the most.'

'And what are the chances of your people being caught?'

'Not more than fifty-fifty.'

'And that's why you've come to me.'

'Yes, sir.'

'Why, exactly?'

'If my people are caught the Soviets could make a diplomatic song and dance about it, and State would be involved.'

'Mr Christianson, I haven't heard a word of what you have told me. I don't want to know. You handle your responsibilities as best you can, and I will handle mine. Good-night, gentlemen.'

And he stood up, turning his back on them as he walked over to a cabinet set in the wall.

Malik sat silently sucking a tooth as Galitsyn summarized the happenings at Peredelkino, his blue eyes on Galitsyn's face, his own face giving no expression of approval or disapproval. When Galitsyn finally ended his report Malik was silent for a few moments before he spoke.

'And now you would like to escort Boyle to East Berlin to sweet-talk the German into handing over his so-called proof?'

'Yes, comrade.'

Malik said softly, 'You are a fool, Galitsyn.'

Galitsyn flushed but said nothing.

'Do you know why you are a fool, my friend?'

'No, comrade.'

Malik leaned forward so that his face was near to Galitsyn's.

'Why do you think that the British chose Boyle to contact the German?'

'I don't know?'

'Did you find that out when he was under the drug?'

'No.'

Malik leaned back grim-faced and tense. 'Let me tell *you* then. This morning we had a report from the embassy in London. Boyle is an intelligence officer. His cover is that he is a barrister. And Lemke worked for him during the war. He controlled Lemke who was working for the Abwehr. We have checked the RSHA records that we captured in Berlin. Lemke was recruited and trained by the Abwehr Aussenstelle at Hamburg, as an agent. He operated back to Hamburg from England until the end of the war. Boyle was his control in London. Your truth-loving Englishman and your sportswriter German are still playing their old games. And they have fooled you, Galitsyn. They are the professionals. You are the innocent.'

Galitsyn's face was white, and his voice unsteady. 'I ask that I am allowed to complete the mission to Berlin, comrade.'

'Why bother, just dispose of the two of them.'

'We need to find out what Lemke was offering as proof to the Americans.'

'They'll run rings round you, comrade.'

'No, comrade. They will not.'

'Galitsyn, you have been through all this charade at Peredelkino. You've been caught up in the play-acting.'

'I wanted Boyle to witness for us. I think he is almost convinced already.'

'I don't care how convinced he is, my friend. I want him buried.'

'And Lemke's so-called proof? We *should* know what it is. If it is to be used by the West it is best that we are fore-armed.'

Malik closed his eyes as he considered what Galitsyn had said. When he opened them his voice was official.

'How long do you want?'

'Ten days. Perhaps two weeks.'

'I'll give you seven. No more.'

CHAPTER EIGHTEEN

It had been a day before Galitsyn had Boyle brought to the office that he was temporarily using in the old HQ. He spent most of that time checking the reports of the surveillance team covering Lemke.

The German seldom went out. A few brief visits to the Budapest Café, a couple of visits to newspaper offices, and one apparently aimless stroll along Karl-Marx-Allee. The girl did all the shopping for food and household goods, and they had followed her to her old rooms and seen the boy Karl go in ten minutes later. This had happened three times since Lemke's return.

The monitoring tapes of his phone calls seemed innocuous. Articles phoned in to newspapers, and negotiations for new assignments. There were no calls to his wife. His mail, too, was solely concerned with business, and none of it was outside East Germany except for a letter of thanks to an editor in Moscow who had apparently helped Lemke on his recent trip. He would have him checked out.

The check on his bank account showed that it was not unusually active. A few hundred marks on deposit and his current account moving in and out of credit by small amounts as cheques were paid in or drawn.

He had photographs of the outside of Lemke's building and the architect's drawings of the floor plan of Lemke's apartment. There had been no possibility of long-range photography of the inside of the apartment, as there were no buildings of a suitable height that overlooked that corner of the apartment block. A man posing as a window-cleaner had planted a small radio-mike with a sucker to the main window but the tapes were made useless by the radio that seemed to play continuously in the room inside.

When Boyle was escorted in, the Russian pointed to a chair on the opposite side of the narrow table. Galitsyn looked without speaking at Boyle's face. Boyle's eyes were alert despite the gaunt cheeks and the cracked lips, and there were those tell-tale tea-leaf spots on the sallow skin that signalled Boyle's age. He was still looking as he spoke.

'Why didn't you tell me, Mr Boyle?'

'Tell you what?'

'That you are an intelligence officer, not a lawyer.'

'I can assure you that I am not an intelligence officer, Colonel Galitsyn.'

'You were a major in the Intelligence Corps during the war, yes?'

'Yes.'

'And Lemke worked for the Abwehr?'

'He worked for the British after he was caught.'

'And you controlled him?'

'Yes.'

'Why did you not tell me this?' Galitsyn said softly.

Boyle shrugged. 'I have no idea what questions you asked me when I was drugged. I was under no obligation to volunteer information to you. But I assure you that I am a lawyer and have been for over thirty years.'

'That I do not believe.'

'You could ask your spies in London to check.'

'They *have* checked.'

'Then they're no good. My court cases are a matter of record.'

'It is easy to substitute a name, Mr Boyle. It is a well-known device.'

Boyle pursed his lips but sat in silence as Galitsyn stared at him.

'If you try to play games with Lemke, my friend, I shall kill you both.'

'The games I shall play will be your games, Galitsyn, not mine.'

Galitsyn pulled over the plan of Lemke's apartment and the photographs of the building. It was nearly two hours later when Galitsyn had finished his briefing.

'He may not co-operate. He said he would only give that proof if his pension was increased.'

Galitsyn shrugged. 'So you increase his pension.'

Boyle looked at the Russian and said softly, 'You want me to betray him. You're not going to let him defect.'

Galitsyn shrugged. 'I can answer that when I know what this so-called evidence is. The Americans can have him. We have no interest in jackals like that.'

'And me? What do you intend for me?'

'You will have helped us, comrade. That will not be forgotten.'

Boyle stared at Galitsyn's face but there was nothing to be read there. The frail camaraderie of Peredelkino had gone.

They flew to Berlin in a small military transport plane, its interior stripped down to the metalwork. There were no seats, and Boyle sat on the floor hunched up against a metal duct, his legs stretched out between two jet engines that were lashed to the floor and being returned to Berlin after major servicing in Kiev. There was no heating, and the temperature was not much above freezing. Despite the blanket they had given him Boyle shivered as the plane swung and lurched on the last fifty miles from Warsaw. They were flying at about three thousand feet, and the squat plane was bucking and sinking as they met the thermals from the hills below.

He could see the lights of a big city spread out below. Long lines of orange stars that marked the main highways, and a necklace of sparkling lights that traced great circles and ran inwards like the spokes of a wheel. They were coming down fast, without airline finesse, almost vertical drops of a few hundred feet at a time until the bright lights of the airport buildings raced under the wings. Then a rough and ready landing, and they were taxiing towards the Aeroflot service hangar.

The navigator had swung back the heavy, metal door and flipped down an aluminium ladder. There was an echoing clanging noise from the hangar, and as Boyle looked out of the single window he saw men working on one of the big Aeroflot airliners.

The hand on his shoulder startled him. It was Galitsyn and he pointed to the door. When he was safely on the tarmac Galitsyn handed down his cases. The air on the ground was warm, and as Boyle stood there with his bag, a black Mercedes limousine pulled up a few yards away. A young man stepped out and walked over to Galitsyn and they both looked across at Boyle as they spoke in Russian. The young man was nodding as Galitsyn spoke. Then he walked across to Boyle.

'I take you to the check-point now, mister.' And he picked up Boyle's bag and carried it to the car. As they turned towards the main terminal Boyle saw the big sign BERLIN–SCHÖNEFELD, and then they were at the side gate, and a Vopo saluted as the red and white poles lifted to let the car through.

The young man spoke without taking his eyes off the road.

'The colonel wishes that you go through all the procedures at check-point Charlie. I take you to the post and wait for you. Is correct that you are on your own. You have booking at Berolina Interhotel in Karl-Marx-Allee. They will ask you of this at check-point because of your luggage. The booking confirmation is in your passport. If they ask you from where you come is from Amsterdam. KLM flight 94 to Tempelhof. Luggage tickets for that flight I fix on your bag.'

The car pulled up silently at a ramshackle old house. Its windows were boarded up but the walls were only a shell. On the opposite side of the street was the high blank face of the Wall. The young man carried his bag down an alleyway past the house, and turned left behind a crumbling brick wall. There was an ancient office, its battered wooden door ajar. The young man pushed the door further open with his foot and held it with his leg outstretched as Boyle went into the shed. In the lights from the street he could see rusting

171

tins on the floor, and clumps of thistles growing through the spokes of an old bicycle wheel.

The young man put down the bag and reached down into the darkness of the far corner. Boyle heard him grunt and then there was a flood of soft light.

'You go down step, sir, to bottom and wait for me.'

Boyle clambered down the six or seven steps of a wooden ladder. He was in a passage that smelled dank and earthy. The walls were rough concrete, the lines from the shuttering still showing from when the concrete was poured.

He followed the young man through the twists and turns of the underground passage for several hundred yards and then there was a set of concrete steps with a wooden handrail. The young man pressed a button and Boyle looked up as a motor whirred and a flap lifted above their heads.

The young man nodded for Boyle to go up the steps. They came up into a small room whose walls were plain, unvarnished pine, with a red telephone on a wooden bracket. The young man had spoken in Russian on the telephone, and as he hung up a small thick-set man had come in through the metal door and the two stood talking. Finally the young man turned to him.

'I fix you labels and you go now through normal checkpoint procedure. This man will be watching. There is taxi for you already with engaged sign at exit point. I leave you now.'

Boyle and the other Russian waited while the tags were tied to Boyle's bag.

As he went through the door he was in the first office on the Soviet side of the check-point, and a uniformed Grenzpolizei man pushed him into the short queue.

He went through all the same procedures that he had gone through a few weeks before, but it seemed like years ago rather than weeks. The night sky was a dark blue, summer sky, and he could see the white floodlights on the Brandenburger Tor. Then he saw the taxi.

The driver asked for no money as they pulled up at the main entrance to the hotel, and a porter carried his bag to the reception counter. He noticed that when he signed the register he was not asked for his passport.

It was a double bedroom with a large sitting-room, pleasant enough; but Boyle sat on the edge of the bed, exhausted, his mind drained of all power to reason. Galitsyn's instructions were clear and precise, and he loathed what he had to do. Put at its best he had to deceive a man in what seemed a good cause. Put at its worst he had to lie, deliberately and coldly, to persuade a man that he was being led to a new life, and then that man would be killed. But before he was killed they wanted to discover what he knew. If what he had said was true he would die; and if it were a pack of lies he would die. And a man who was to be one of Her Majesty's judges would weave the elaborate network of deception that would lead him to his death. As if triggered by his thoughts he lifted the bag on to the bed beside him, and snapped open the locks. The big, brown envelope was on top of his clothes. He opened the flap and emptied the contents on to the bed-cover.

There was a United States passport in the names of Orville Lundgren and Ursula Lundgren, Social Security cards, a thousand dollars in cash, credit cards on First National Bank and Exxon. A photograph of an apartment at Marina del Rey, a driving licence, a receipt in the name of Lundgren for a year's rental of the apartment, and a bank deposit statement showing a 30,000 dollar credit in the Lundgren name. He slid them all back haphazardly into the envelope and walked over to the window.

He could just see Lemke's apartment block, and he wondered if the German was also tense and impatient, waiting for the radio signal. He thought of the letter that had lain on his desk at his chambers that day, offering him a judgeship. If only he had not taken Parker's phone call. Or perhaps the fatal step had been the moment when he had agreed to help them. Perhaps it went even further back to the day when he had walked up the stairs at the dingy house in Croydon to arrest Lemke.

He sensed now that he was doomed. Not necessarily to

death, but his flawed pattern seemed to have smashed a lifetime's solidity. More than thirty years of hard work and indifference to the pleasures of life had been destroyed in a few days. Maybe his fate had been decided even before the house in Croydon. If Lemke had not been picked up and used by the Abwehr. Or if Lemke's mother had not been a tart. He sighed aloud at the impossible genetic trail that twisted and turned in his confused mind. He shuddered as he remembered that Galitsyn and his men would be watching his every move until the drama was played out.

Boyle suddenly felt a flush of anger. Whatever had been the start-point he had done nothing to deserve this fate. He had offended against no commandment, no law; he had claimed no unjust reward. Indeed, he had claimed no reward of any kind. His fees even had not been spent on self-indulgencies. No Manets or Rembrandts, no stocks or shares, no mistress, no family. He had made no demands on society and only the most slender demands on life itself. What had gone wrong? Of what sin was this the wages?

As he looked across the roof-tops the lights of the city were blurred, he could feel a heavy pulse beating in his neck, and for a moment he held the frame of the window to steady himself as the room moved slowly and barely perceptibly under his feet.

He shuffled unsteadily back to the bed, his arms half outstretched to keep his balance. As the backs of his legs touched the bed he covered himself with the sheet and lay back. His eyes closed and he was asleep in seconds.

Galitsyn used the pass-key to go into Boyle's suite when there was no answer to his knocking, and he stood looking down at the figure on the bed. Boyle looked even older than his years; beads of perspiration on his sallow face, the mouth agape, the breathing stertorous, and his hands clasped on his thin chest as if he were already dead. The old man stirred slowly as Galitsyn shook him by the shoulder, and then leaned up on one elbow shading his eyes from the early morning light.

Galitsyn sat watching and talking, as Boyle washed and shaved and changed his clothes; going over the scenario again and again. Probing the threads of the story and checking Boyle's responses to unexpected questions. When Boyle was dressed and ready, Galitsyn had pointed to the phone. It had to go on, but he reckoned that Boyle was very near the end of his tether. The strength of character that had been evident during the early days of interrogation had crumbled away, and what was left was a shell that a man like Lemke could crack if he once sensed that Boyle was lying. If Malik could see Boyle now he would know that there was no question of him still being an intelligence officer. Messenger yes. But nothing more.

Boyle dialled the number and waited. He recognized Lemke's voice immediately.

'On the twelfth day of Christmas my true love sent to me . . .'

There was a silence, and then Lemke's voice whispered, *'Um Gottes willen. Wer ist dass?'*

Boyle glanced quickly at Galitsyn, who nodded.

'This is Boyle. I've come to see you.'

'What's wrong? Where are you?'

'I'm at the Berolina. I'm coming round to see you.'

'No. No. I'll come and see you at the hotel.'

'Come right away.'

'OK.'

Galitsyn glanced briefly around the room and then moved to the empty suite next to Boyle's. He telephoned the KGB special signals unit to check that the microphones in Boyle's rooms were live and being recorded. Then he pressed his portable microphone, with its suction pad to the wall, and pulled up a chair. He looped the thin flexible wire and hung it on the arm of the chair as he put the plastic-covered amplifier to his ear.

The hall-porter phoned to announce that Lemke was in the foyer and Boyle asked them to send him up.

Lemke's smooth, healthy face, and his casual clothes,

seemed to bring some strange normality to the meeting, and Boyle waved him to one of the tapestry chairs.

'What's wrong?' Lemke asked as he sat down.

'Nothing's wrong, Otto. On the contrary I've got good news for you. They've agreed to the increase in your ... er ... in your pension.'

'You don't look very happy about it.'

'I've been very busy on your account, Otto.'

'Tell me.'

'Like I said, they have agreed to the increase, in exchange for the information you offered.'

Lemke looked at Boyle, his leg swinging nonchalantly and his jaw cradled in his left hand.

'What's wrong, Boyle?'

'Nothing. Why should anything be wrong?'

'God knows, but you look uneasy to me.'

'Just tired out, my friend.'

'When did you leave Moscow?'

'About a couple of days after you. Why did you just disappear without warning?'

'I don't give warnings, my friend. I go when it seems time to go.'

'Are you ready to go now?'

'I thought I was to wait for the code on the radio.'

'That's been changed.'

'Why?'

'We've found an easier way.'

'Tell me.'

'You can go through the check-point ...'

'Never, my friend, I told you.'

'With a United States passport and full documentation.'

For the first time Lemke's eyes showed interest.

'Where are they?'

Boyle pointed to his case.

'They're here.'

'Can I see them?'

'You can't have them until I have your information.'

'I didn't say can I *have* them, I said can I see them.'

Boyle stood up and bent over the case, snapping open the locks and lifting the lid. He pulled out the brown envelope.

He sat back in his chair and handed the envelope to Lemke who opened the flap and looked in cautiously. He looked back at Boyle's face and handed back the envelope.

'You take them out.'

Boyle shrugged and bent down, letting the contents slide to the floor.

Starting with the passport, Lemke picked up the items one by one. Laying them on the chair next to his, after scrutinizing each piece carefully. Looking at the photograph he said, 'Is this the place they've taken for me?'

'Yes. The receipt for the first year's rental is in there.'

'I saw it.'

'When can you show me the extra material?'

Lemke looked towards the window as if he were considering Boyle's question. Then, as if he had made a decision, he turned his head to look at Boyle's face.

'Bring this stuff . . .' He waved his hand over the pile of documents on the chair beside him, ' . . . to my place this evening about seven. I'll give you the information. How do you intend getting me out?'

'When we decide the day for you to leave I shall arrange for somebody to come through with a similar passport, a replica, and you will go back in his place.'

'What happens to him?'

'Leave that to us, Otto.'

'When can we go?'

'One day after I have the extra information.'

'What if you are not satisfied with it?'

'It is not for me to judge. We shall take you out as promised. The extra information only affects what you're paid.'

'What about my girl?'

'A girl will come through on the same passport.'

'What happens the other side of the check-point?'

'Somebody will be waiting for you.'

'How'd you get here?'

'I flew from Amsterdam.'

'How'd you get to Amsterdam?'

'The flight started in Dublin, I picked it up in London.'

Lemke stood up slowly. 'OK. We shall see you at seven, then.'

'Right. I'll be there.'

Lemke held out his hand, and Boyle hesitated only for a moment before he took it.

He watched from the window and saw Lemke cross the wide road. The German turned and stood for a moment looking up at the hotel windows. Then he turned away and moved off.

Galitsyn went back into Boyle's suite as soon as Lemke had cleared the hotel.

'You've got to go more slowly, Boyle. He's very edgy. It's almost as if he suspects something. Why didn't he give you back the check-words when you gave him the code phrase on the telephone?'

'I don't know. But the code was only for use in Moscow. He was probably scared when he heard it used here.'

'You're sure of that, Boyle?' Galitsyn's eyes were hard with suspicion.

'You mean did I give him some warning?'

'Exactly.'

'No. I didn't warn him.'

'Why not?'

'I told you, Galitsyn, that I was almost convinced that the explosion was an accident. I told you that I would help you with Lemke.'

'Why do you help me?'

'Because I believe that the consequences would be unthinkable if the Soviet people were told that the explosion was deliberate. That's why I want to help you.'

'What if it were true?'

Boyle shook his head. 'We have discussed this enough, Colonel. You must leave it to me now.'

'I warn you,' said Galitsyn, jabbing the air with his finger, 'I warn you. Don't play games.'

'Is there no one you trust, Galitsyn?'

'No. There is not. And who do you trust, comrade?'

Boyle pursed his lips. 'Can you let me have some money, Colonel? I want to go for a walk and maybe have a coffee away from this place.'

'There's money in the drawer beside your bed, comrade. You'll be watched of course.'

Autenowski had fetched Kempski down from the CIA detachment in Hamburg. Kempski was an experienced field officer who spoke both German and Russian,

They had gone through check-point Charlie with the two girls, then to the café in Alexander Platz, and on to the safe-house in Heinz Beimler Strasse.

At two o'clock all four of them had strolled down to Karl-Marx-Allee. Almost opposite Lemke's block was a State betting shop and a small café and bar.

As they ate at the table by the window the two men sat opposite the girls so that one or another could watch Lemke's place. They spotted the yellow van parked on the side-street and assumed, from the reports that they had read from their people in East Berlin, that the van was part of the KGB surveillance.

Kempski said softly, 'I can't see the registration number but there's a gap in the canvas hood. 'I'd guess that's for a camera.'

Autenowski nodded. 'I'll go next door to the betting shop to spin out the time.'

He pushed back his chair, smiled at the waitress and reached for the copy of the *Berliner Zeitung* and turned to the sports pages. He found a few runners tipped for the last meeting that day in Dresden and dropped the paper on the nearest table.

It was twenty minutes later when he came back and he was barely settled in his chair when Kempski said out of the corner of her mouth, 'Look. Just crossing over.'

'Jesus wept. What the hell's going on.' And he stood up again and hurried out on to the wide street. It was the Englishman all right. Walking very slowly past the entrance to

Lemke's apartment block. His shoulders bent and his feet scraping along as if he were suffering from some senile disease. Instinctively Autenowski moved his arm to check the reassuring shape of the gun in his shoulder holster. He glanced back at the restaurant and saw Kempski paying the bill, the girls standing, ready to move off. He watched Boyle pass the KGB van and head towards Alexander Platz, and then Kempski and the girls had joined him.

'You follow him, Kempski, he might recognize me. Toni and I will keep an eye on this place. I'll send her back to the safe-house in an hour.' He checked his watch. 'She'll be there at 5.20.'

Kempski had walked off with the other girl and Toni had linked her arm in Autenowski's as she smiled up at his face. 'There's a guy in a blue check shirt been watching us for the last few minutes. Don't look now but he's looking in the hairdresser's shop window.'

'OK. Just keep walking.'

They walked about ten yards when Autenowski released the girl's arm and bent down to do up his shoe-laces. As he straightened up he glanced back down the street and then moved on with the girl.

'He's watching Lemke's place. They're really clamping down on him. We'll have to go in for him tonight.'

A few minutes later they turned and walked back again, past Lemke's place, the café, and on towards Strausberger Platz. The man who had been watching them was hovering near the yellow van with his back towards them.

Then it was time for the girl to go back to the safe-house and Autenowski went back to the café and ordered a beer.

Fifteen minutes later the yellow van was driven off and it was replaced a few minutes later by a larger, dark-green Public Works lorry with the East German bear emblem on its sides. The driver sat for a few moments and then got out and walked to the back of the vehicle. He climbed up inside, swung the doors to, and didn't reappear.

Kempski came back alone, and Autenowski ordered more beer as Kempski sat down at the table.

'He's staying at the Beroliner at the other end of Karl-Marx. I went up in the elevator with him. He's in Room 507. It's a suite, and there was a KGB man hanging around in the corridor trying to look like a floor-service waiter. He didn't check Boyle, but he looked me over and phoned down to the lobby. He was speaking Russian but I couldn't hear what he said. I walked down the stairs and there were two guys watching the elevators. Boyle's working with them, that's for sure.'

'For God's sake, how do you turn a top English attorney and get him to work for the KGB?'

'Pump him full of drugs. Put the frighteners on him. Threaten his family.'

'He hasn't got a family.'

'OK, you frighten *him*.'

'To do what?'

'Who knows, buddy. But I know what we've got to do.'

'What?'

'Knock him off, and quick.'

'The British will raise hell with Langley.'

'So how do they find out? They told us he was either in the Lubyanka or out at Peredelkino. They won't even know he's gone. Anyway, they'll blame the Soviets.'

'They'll find out sooner or later.'

'Let 'em. They let Philby do a flit long after we warned them. They'll let this bastard give them the slip too.'

'Maybe the British do know. Maybe they're playing some game of their own.'

'So let's stop 'em.'

'We'll have to do it tonight.'

'It'll have to be straight in and out then. The hotel's crawling with KGB.'

'The check-point will be closed by the time we're through. We'll have to wait overnight.'

'No way. We'll do it early. The girls can hire a taxi at the place by Alexander Platz and wait for us. We can be at Charlie in six minutes easily.'

'OK. Let's get back to the house.'

Autenowski was behind Kempski otherwise Boyle would have seen them as he walked down the hotel steps to the street. It was 6.45 and the two Americans had intended to be in Boyle's room by 7 o'clock.

Kempski put out his arm to stop Autenowski, and then turned to block him off from Boyle's line of sight. He said softly, 'Just talk to me. Anything. Boyle's just come out of the hotel. Look over my shoulder and tell me when he's clear of us. He walks very slowly so there's no hurry.'

'Are you sure it was Boyle?'

'Quite sure.'

'Was he alone?'

'Yep.'

Autenowski said slowly, 'He's well clear of us now. He's going towards the café. Probably going to see friend Lemke.'

'OK. Let's go.'

They strolled slowly down Karl-Marx-Allee and the broad street was crowded now. It was a Saturday evening and somewhere in the distance they could hear a military band playing 'Wiener Blut'. They were probably giving a concert at the Brandenburger Tor.

Kempski said quietly, 'I reckon he's going to visit Lemke. Look, he's watching the traffic so that he can cross.'

'We'll have to wait until he comes out. We can't do anything in broad daylight with all these people around. It might be dark when he leaves, otherwise we do it when he gets back to the hotel.'

'OK. I'll go back to stop the girls. I'll tell them we'll be staying overnight.'

'I'll go in the café and keep an eye on this place.'

Boyle walked inside the small hallway and up the stone steps to the second floor. There were two doors side by side, and number 15 was on the left. He pressed the bell and waited.

All his carefully rehearsed dialogue was forgotten when

the girl opened the door. It was like being switched back in time. She was just like the first girl that Lemke had had at the house on Limpsfield Chart. The same knowing prettiness, her full young breasts thrusting invitingly, and the same long shapely legs. And when his eyes went back from her breasts to her face she was smiling. An amused, aware smile, and the sexual invitation in the blue eyes was unmistakable. She looked at his face and her pink tongue moved across her lips.

'*Was willst du.*' Her voice was soft and surprisingly gentle.

'*Ich suche Herr Lemke, bitte.*'

She smiled '*Komm' herein.*'

And Boyle flushed as his body touched hers as she barely moved after waving him inside. She nodded.'*Er ist im Wohnzimmer, Herr Boyle.*'

And there was Lemke, sitting comfortably on a settee, a drink in his hand, and a bottle and glasses on the coffee table in front of him.

'A Scotch, my friend? The real thing, especially for you.'

'A very small one, then.' In Lemke's own place the lies were going to be even more degrading, and he tried to avoid looking at the room.

The girl sat beside Lemke and she poured a drink for Boyle and herself. Boyle put the brown envelope on the floor beside his chair and lifted his glass.

'Cheers.'

Lemke said nothing, and unsmiling he lifted his glass.

'You brought the documentation, Mr Boyle?'

'Yes.'

'Now what?'

'You hand over the other evidence that you offered.'

'They were very interested in that?'

'It wasn't discussed with me. I was only told to hand over the documentation in exchange for the information.'

'What would happen if I decided to keep the information until I was across the border?'

'Nothing. We have agreed to that, and the only difference

would be that we should go back to the original financial arrangements.'

Lemke smiled. 'Don't worry, Mr Boyle. They'll get what they want in the end.'

'In the end?'

'Maybe here in Berlin, or maybe when we are all in Washington.' He put his arm round the girl. 'And now you have met Ushi what do you think of her?'

'I think she's very pretty, Otto. I'm sure you will be very happy together.'

'Unfortunately she doesn't speak English. But that's all to the good. We can talk freely together.' And suddenly Boyle noticed that Lemke's hand had moved so that it was cupping the girl's breast, his fingers squeezing the big mound and his thumb casually teasing its tip. When he looked back at Lemke's face the German was smiling.

'D'you remember the girls you arranged, my friend?'

Boyle was silent, but Lemke's smile only broadened.

'She told me. The little Irish girl. She told me about what happened the night you gave me the drug to make me sleep.'

'I don't remember that.'

Lemke laughed softly. 'I remember. I didn't believe her at first, but she showed me the marks. She said she thought you'd never stop. She said you were like a dog on a bitch.'

Boyle's voice shook. 'I'm afraid she was lying.'

Lemke shook his head still smiling. 'We were both young men in those days. She'd have let you have her every day, you know. She was quite disappointed.' Lemke leaned forward to pour himself another drink.

'D'you know what's the matter with you, Boyle?'

Boyle was silent.

'You're too closed in. What the Americans call up-tight. Tell me . . .' he said ' . . . how many girls have you screwed since that night?'

'I'm not married, Mr Lemke.'

Lemke grinned. 'How many, Boyle? Half a dozen? Three? Two? None? Maybe I should find you a girl before we leave. How about that?'

184

'When do you want to leave?'

Lemke shrugged. 'As soon as possible.'

'Show me the new material and we could go tonight.'

Lemke shook his head. 'Don't be impatient, Boyle. Your people can wait another day or so.'

'It's a question of security, and a man standing by with a girl to make the inward crossing.'

Lemke looked at Boyle reflectively, his left hand fondling the girl's breast, his right hand beside him. His brown eyes were suddenly hard.

'Why did you do it, Boyle?'

'Do what?'

'Change sides, you bastard.'

'I don't know what you mean.'

'You know what I mean, all right. You just don't know how I knew.'

'You'd better explain what you mean.'

'You're shaking, Boyle. You're frightened.' Lemke took his arm from around the girl and leaned forward.

'How did you know when I left Moscow, Boyle?'

'I didn't say I did know.'

'Don't give me that shit, comrade. You said you left Moscow a couple of days after I left. How the hell do you know *when* I left?'

'I assumed you left the day we last met.'

'Why do you assume that? Just because I don't see you doesn't mean that I've left. I could be lying low. I could have had other things to do. For all you know I could have left only two days ago.'

Boyle shrugged. 'So I made a wrong assumption.'

'The bloody Russians told you when I left. You must be working for them.'

Boyle shook his head and then swallowed convulsively as he saw Lemke's hand come up from the settee. It was pointing a gun at him. A Luger.

'Now you tell *me*, Boyle. This time it's you that's on the wrong side, not me.'

And then the door-bell rang.

185

Lemke looked towards the door then back at Boyle.

'What's going on?'

'I don't know.'

Lemke saw the fear in Boyle's eyes and was sure it wasn't to do with him. He turned to the girl. 'See who it is. I'm not available.' He tucked the pistol back down the side of the cushion.

They heard a man speaking in German but with a heavy Silesian accent. There was a collection for handicapped children, would they be kind enough to give something? The girl came back in.

'*Zwei Mark, bitte, für die kinder . . .*'

'Don't let him in.'

'I've put the chain on the door.'

And as she said it they heard the chain snap, and there was a draught from the outer door.

Galitsyn pushed open the door, and his eyes took in the room. The girl had disappeared into the bedroom. As Lemke rose from the settee Galitsyn thrust him back with one hand, and without turning he said, 'Has he given you the information, Boyle?'

Boyle couldn't bring himself to answer. To deceive Lemke was one thing; to sell him out to his face was too much. He heard Lemke scream as Galitsyn's hand grabbed his hair and pulled back his head. Lemke's hand came up with the Luger and he heard Galitsyn's indrawn breath.

'You bastard. You bloody German bastard.'

And Boyle saw that Lemke had managed to get to his feet. Then the Russian's hand had slammed edge-on across Lemke's mouth and Galitsyn had him against the wall.

'Where . . . is . . . the . . . evidence?'

Galitsyn had his hands round the German's throat and he crashed his head against the wall.

'Where . . . is . . . it?'

Boyle shouted, 'There is no information, Galitsyn. I'm sure of it.'

Galitsyn was oblivious to Boyle's shout, and again and again he crashed the German's head against the wall. A picture fell to the ground and the girl was screaming in the bedroom. But Galitsyn was beyond stopping now. Lemke's eyes were closed, and blood poured from his mouth and nose over the Russian's hands and wrists. There was a sickening hollow sound as the German's head crashed against the wall a dozen times. Then suddenly, as if somebody had pressed a button, Galitsyn stopped, and Lemke's body slid gently to the floor. Boyle had no doubt that he was already dead.

The Russian turned to look at Boyle, his face flushed, his chest heaving and his hands still flexing as if they were still round the German's throat.

'Are you sure he had nothing, Boyle? Did he admit that he had nothing?'

'No. But I'm sure he didn't. It became obvious.'

'I shall hear it all on the tapes, you know.'

The door from the bedroom opened and the girl stood there, her long blonde hair awry, her face drained of blood. Boyle saw Galitsyn look at her, his eyes going from the pretty face to the firm young breasts and Boyle knew in that instant what was in the Russian's mind.

Galitsyn walked over to the girl and stared at her face, his hands on his hips, still breathing heavily. Then he opened the bedroom door and pushed her inside. He closed the door and turned, walking slowly back to Boyle.

'It's finished here. You come with me, Boyle.'

There were no lights on the stairs and Boyle followed Galitsyn down, his hand touching the wall to keep his balance as he tested each step on the way.

At the bottom of the stairs, in the small entrance the evening sun cast rectangles of golden light on the mosaic floor from the doors to the street. Then from the darkness behind the stairs Boyle saw a dark figure, its hand raised to strike at Galitsyn, and as his mouth opened to warn him he heard a noise like a tyre being punctured and felt a pain at the back of his head, and then a blow in his back.

Kempski and Autenowski had been waiting at the foot of

the stairs, and were out on the street two hundred yards down Karl-Marx-Allee towards Alexander Platz, before the men had poured out of the green lorry and headed for Lemke's place.

The girls were waiting for them, with the taxi, and they were at check-point Charlie about ten minutes later.

The two girls and Kempski were already through the barrier to the Allied Zone, and Autenowski only needed the final clearance when the bell rang and the Russian guard picked up the telephone. As he hung up he walked to the red and white pole, and waving his arms, he shouted at the queue: '*Aller zurück. Niemand geht weiter.*'

Autenowski waved his passport at the guard and pointed to the two girls and Kempski. The guard looked at the three and then back at Autenowski. '*Nix, Amerikaner, du bleibst hier.*' And he coughed as Autenowski shot him twice as he went under the pole.

For a moment there was silence, then a sub-machine-gun was firing at the four figures racing for the shop on the corner. A US Army truck pulled across in front of the pole and took a couple of dozen bullets along its length. Someone shouted to the guards to stop firing, and there was a strange silence, until from far away came the sound of two police sirens, and very faintly on the evening breeze, the strains of 'The Red Flag' as the band ended its Saturday concert.

Galitsyn had been unconscious for two hours from the blow to his head, and when he awoke he felt the bandage tight round his head. Despite the doctor's orders he had gone down to the casualty bay.

Boyle's body was still on the trolley, face down, and there were massive plasters across the back of his shaven skull and a few inches from his spine. He read the medical card slowly and carefully. The unidentified casualty had been dead on arrival. Two lead-nosed slugs had been removed, one from the base of the skull and one from the back of the rib-cage. Death had been instantaneous due to massive destruction of vital organs by the bullets. The two slugs had been handed over to the Volkspolizei Forensic Department. Lemke's body was already at the morgue.

Malik had done the negotiating himself with the Military Attaché at the British Embassy, and had handed over the two flattened slugs in a small plastic bag. Despite their distortion from striking solid bone, the criss-cross file marks were still visible and Malik had slid across his desk a set of photographs of similarly marked spent slugs. They were carefully annotated with the names of men whose circumstances of death would be known to the British. And known to be CIA victims.

Boyle was buried privately in the quiet churchyard in Limpsfield Parish Church with only the minister and Parker in attendance.

The science correspondents and military experts of the three serious Sundays had been briefed along with their counterparts at *The Times* and the *Daily Telegraph*. It was an 'unofficial' briefing and the documents were laid out on a table for them to see. They were told the parameters within which they could write, and left to get on with it.

By agreement they held over the stories until they had done a little checking themselves, and when they finally went to print the material was merely incorporated in general articles about the world problem of nuclear waste. The Soviet Union had denied that any such explosion took place and a number of western scientists stated that they were more inclined to the Soviet statement.

The story was the second item in a three-item Panorama, and out of five letters to *The Times* only two were considered worth publishing. Neither editors nor the public were all that interested in the story, and it barely made a paragraph after five days.

In the following year's Honours List a Leonard H. Parker was awarded an MBE 'for services to the Foreign Office'. In the United States, William Voytek Autenowski was transferred to the CIA detachment in Toronto without upgrading. In Moscow, Galitsyn can be seen most days by travellers landing at Sheremetyevo, where he is the major in charge of airport security. Even at this moment, somewhere in Moscow, London and Washington, three other men will be planning and mounting some similar operation.

As someone once said, 'Give a man a flag, and a white horse, and starting a war is easy.'

THE WORLD'S GREATEST THRILLER WRITERS
NOW AVAILABLE IN GRANADA PAPERBACKS

Len Deighton

Twinkle, Twinkle, Little Spy	£1.50	☐
Yesterday's Spy	£1.50	☐
Spy Story	£1.50	☐
Horse Under Water	£1.50	☐
Billion Dollar Brain	£1.50	☐
The Ipcress File	£1.50	☐
An Expensive Place to Die	£1.50	☐
Declarations of War	£1.25	☐
Close-Up	£1.50	☐
SS-GB	£1.50	☐
XPD	£1.95	☐

Ted Allbeury

The Only Good German	85p	☐
Moscow Quadrille	75p	☐
The Man With the President's Mind	85p	☐
The Lantern Network	85p	☐
The Reaper	£1.25	☐
Consequence of Fear	£1.25	☐

All these books are available at your local bookshop or newsagent, or can be ordered direct from the publisher. Just tick the titles you want and fill in the form below.

Name _____

Address _____

_____

Write to Granada Cash Sales
PO Box 11, Falmouth, Cornwall TR10 9EN.

Please enclose remittance to the value of the cover price plus:

UK 45p for the first book, 20p for the second book plus 14p per copy for each additional book ordered to a maximum charge of £1.63.

BFPO and Eire 45p for the first book, 20p for the second book plus 14p per copy for the next 7 books, thereafter 8p per book.

Overseas 75p for the first book and 21p for each additional book.

Granada Publishing reserve the right to show new retail prices on covers, which may differ from those previously advertised in the text or elsewhere.
GF1681